Blue Ridge High

A Novel
by
Ed Buhrer

PublishAmerica
Baltimore

© 2004 by Ed Buhrer.
All rights reserved. No part of this book may be reproduced, stored in a retrieval system or transmitted in any form or by any means without the prior written permission of the publishers, except by a reviewer who may quote brief passages in a review to be printed in a newspaper, magazine or journal.

First printing

ISBN: 1-4137-4646-2
PUBLISHED BY PUBLISHAMERICA, LLLP
www.publishamerica.com
Baltimore

Printed in the United States of America

This is a work of fiction. Some of the places are real; others are not. All characters are the creation of the author, and any resemblance to persons, both living and dead, is purely coincidental and unintentional.

What some readers of the author's first novel, *LURAY*, had to say...

"Wow! A former student of this author bought me a copy of *LURAY* for Christmas. What a treat! I started reading it on December 26th and couldn't put it down. Read it in three hours or so, with only one bathroom break and time out for lunch. Great dialogue, delightful love story, nice subplots, and believeable characters. Loved the detail in the description, all the food, and the idea of calling a mountain "Mom!" As I said, what a treat! I want more from Ed Buhrer!"
- Trish, Pennsylvania

"The story kept me so captivated that I couldn't put this book down!...I hope more is coming from this author! I can't seem to find anything else by him, but I hope he's writing something else. Characters were real, the dialogue was authentic, description super, and I loved the love story. Great novel!"
- Ina, Colorado

"Best book I've read in three years...*LURAY* kept me turning page after page. I would keep getting to within a couple pages of the end of a chapter and figure on stopping there, but then the end of that chapter would make me want to start the next. The next thing I knew I was finished with it! This author has a great flair for realistic dialogue, great descriptions (without going overboard), characters you want to know, and he makes you want to fall in love all over again. I hope more of this author's books are out there because my wife and I are waiting for them. I was only disappointed once: when the book ended!"
- Ted, Connecticut

"Okay, when's the sequel coming? You can't just stop with Tom and Sandi there…a great read--fast, vivid, illuminating, a real page-turner. I felt like I was there in Luray, with Tom (and all the rest) ALL THE TIME! And if that Wild Bill character is based on a real guy, I've got to meet him. Ed Buhrer writes about people: they are real, their speech is real, and you actually care about them. This author says it all the way it ought to be said. Great book and I want the sequel fast!"
    - Richard, Chicago

"*LURAY* is captivating, enjoyable, hilarious, honest, and heart-warming. I was stuck between wanting to read it in one sitting and not wanting it to end. The characters were easy to love (especially Tom). It's the mark of a great novel when the reader feels like she is a part of the story line and she becomes emotionally involved…The technique he used to depict the way people from Luray speak was brilliant; the country dialect really completed Becky's character. His portrayal of the Blue Ridge was so descriptive that I could picture the great mountains rising against the amber sky as Tom spent most of his evenings enjoying the last remnants of the day on his back porch. He also described Tom's cabin and classroom so well that I felt as though I was the person walking into the modest bedroom…I can honestly say that I enjoyed every word of this novel."
    - Mary Beth, Virginia

"*LURAY* is an exceptional book from start to finish. Buhrer captures the feel of small town life and creates a story that connects with anyone who has ever truly fallen in love. His style of writing is a breath of fresh air and reminds me of some of the great authors of the past who were more interested in putting the reader in the story, vs. the new age of authors who want to put their story in the theaters. The author's humor made this a very enjoyable read and his attention to detail really made me feel like I was seeing, hearing, smelling, and feeling what Tom was living in Luray. Bravo to Buhrer and I hope to see more works like *LURAY* in the near future!"
   - Soupy, North Carolina

"The two hundred pages seemed more like fifty. I intended to take *LURAY* with me next week on vacation to read in increments during the car ride to my destination and back. Today I devoured the entire book in a few hours. I could only set it down long enough to go to the bathroom and get a snack. I have never before read a book that kept me intrigued through every chapter, every page, and every word that I read."
   - Andrea, Virginia

Dedicated to

my students, who have
kept me young all these years

and

"Wild Bill" Hinek, who left us
too soon

teaching (n.) – the act of dedicating one's life to the most unappreciated, the most underpaid, the most overworked, the least understood, and the most important and vital profession in our society.

ignorance (n.) – the condition of lacking knowledge of some kind.

stupidity (n.) – the condition of being ignorant and not wishing to change that condition.

irony (n.) – "naming the international airport in Washington, D.C. for the president who fired all the air-traffic controllers" – unknown lesbian comic

Luray (p.n.) – a nice place to be (most of the time, with most of the people)

redneck (n.) – slang. a person whose family has completely ignored the normal pattern of evolution; one who could be the poster person for the anti-inbreeding movement; usually distinguished by the wearing of a dirty cap with some kind of company logo.

hypocrite (n.) – what the most loudly self-declared Southern "good Christian" is.

love (n.) – something you understand only after falling into it so hard, so deeply, and so intensely that it can consume all thoughts and actions.

…and so it goes…

1

The sun was peeking over the top of Mom, our backyard mountain, spreading gold slowly down along the tops of the bare trees and evergreens, when Sandi nudged me seconds before the clock radio was due to go off.

"I'm up," I told her, swinging my legs out from under the covers.

"Lemme get to the bathroom first, though. I've got that 8:00 class. Go make the coffee," she said, sliding herself, naked, out of bed.

"You know, I could wake up to that for only another fifty years," I murmured.

"Well, it's not gonna look like this fifty years from now, sweetie, so enjoy the view for now," she said, disappearing into the bathroom and closing the door.

I did.

Our cozy little cabin had a chill in the air that mid-February morning. We'd burned some oak in the fireplace the evening before and had turned the heat down below seventy. We'd discovered that we both preferred cold to hot, even in the winter, and liked sleeping in human balls, curled up against one another under a blanket and quilt.

I turned the thermostat to seventy-two to cut the chill quickly and padded my way into the tiny kitchen and began fiddling with the grinder and some coffee beans. By the time the coffeemaker had started gurgling, Sandi had emerged from the john.

"You know, you are really unique," I told her as I headed for my turn in the "throne room."

"Whaddya mean?" she asked with a slight frown and a single raised eyebrow.

"You've got to be the only woman in the world who can get done in the bathroom in under an hour."

"Well, it helps that I don't wear any make-up, y'know," she observed.

"Yeah," I answered, closing the door.

Part of the way through the second half of my first year of teaching in Page County, Virginia, a lot had happened in my life since I'd driven Baby, my inherited '69 Camaro Z-28, down from the Pittsburgh area, over the Blue Ridge and Skyline Drive, into Luray.

I'd begun to learn the tools of what would be my life's work, teaching—or trying to—high-school juniors and seniors; I'd gotten caught up in a murder-kidnapping, enough to experience my Andy Warhol fifteen minutes' of fame; most importantly, I'd quickly fallen in love with a blond goddess named Sandi and had proposed at Christmas with my mom's engagement ring. Oh, yeah, Pop had come up from his recent retirement in Florida to escape from my Aunt Hildy for a week, had fallen in love with Sandi's mother, and in July, when Sandi and I were scheduled to hook up to one another in a simple ceremony, my father was soon to become my father-in-law as well. As I said, a lot had happened in half a year.

I kissed her goodbye as she started the Mustang and drove down the gravel driveway, beeping three times to help Becky wake Ronnie up. Since I'd started driving her younger sister to school with me, poor Ronnie'd had to get up almost an hour earlier than when one of her friends had picked her up in the fall. She'd kept threatening to go back to that routine so she could get the extra sack time, but liked telling me that she "didn't want to deprive you of my entertaining conversations every morning and afternoon." On the days I stayed late or had meetings, she still caught rides home with Rachel.

I watched until I saw the light come on in Ronnie's bedroom, then went back in for my second and last cup of coffee. I liked Tuesdays and Thursdays better; Sandi's first class in her last semester at JMU wasn't until ten on those days, so we had a little more time in the morning to sit and talk…or make love. Still, I was glad she was back in school, finishing her final semester, one that she'd postponed for several years until she'd been able to put some demons to rest…and to fall in love with me.

Twenty minutes later, Ronnie's knock told me it was time to hop into Baby and head for another Monday at Mountain Valley High.

Remnants of a recent snow still lingered in hollows and shaded spots along 340 as I drove between the farm fields and the two parallel ranges of the Blue Ridge.

"What're we gonna do in Creative Writing this week?" Ronnie asked, her blond hair constantly falling in her face.

"Thought I'd have you start writing and then film your own videos, commercials sellin' something," I replied. "Remember? It was on the syllabus that you never looked at."

"I did!" she chirped, "but you expect me to remember something I read back in September?!"

"You're supposed to look at it more than that one time, dummy," I told her in a stage growl.

"Awright already! We're not even at school yet, so stop teachin'!" she grumbled, looking out her window. "Commercials for what?" she asked a few seconds later.

"Up to you. Only thing I'm gonna tell you is you have to sell something. I want you to do a parody of some commercial you've already seen. You've already learned what a parody is an' I showed you *Monty Python and the Holy Grail*. Now I want you to demonstrate that you can write one, too."

"Can we do it with other kids or do we hafta do it by ourselves?"

"Either, but no more than three kids on one commercial."

"Oh, cool! This is gonna be *so* cool!" she said, settling into a brighter mood. If I haven't mentioned it before, Ronnie is definitely *not* a "morning person," although she's been working at it.

Don't get me wrong; I love my future sister-in-law, and I've watched a slowly developing maturity in her, but Ronnie is one of those adolescents who needs to get out of high school and away from Page County in order to begin to bloom on her own. I think she knows that, too; at first, all her talk about going to Virginia Tech centered mostly around just getting out of Page County (*"it's boring, there's nothing to do"*), but now, I think she's noticed and realized that some of her peers—kids she's been in school with forever—are heading in directions that Ronnie has no interest in…or they are not heading anywhere and think that life is going to take care of itself for them. Ronnie's smart, and smarter than that, and between Sandi and her mom, Ronnie has a pretty good sense of what goals she needs to pursue.

Of course, she's not unique; a lot of my seniors are already on their way to the next stage; most of the rest are getting there, but a handful will probably spend the rest of their lives in the county. The boys who only lived for baseball season and summer leagues will use their connections to find jobs in the local factories making doors or in the few retail businesses; on the weekends, they'll join their fathers, sitting around with beers, talking about their own baseball "glory days"; I've noticed that Page County has more than its share of forty-year-old boys who found undemanding high-school girlfriends to marry, girls too scared or insecure to leave their own personal comfort zones and who now spend more time away from their husbands than with them, going "antiquing" or quilting or weaving baskets together in little social clusters, wondering why they married who they did. You can recognize them in Wal-Mart by the downward curves on either side of their mouths.

We had the same kids back in Pennsylvania when I was in high school, just not as many. Most of us were busting to get out and prove to the world that we needed to see all of it; anyway, our parents didn't expect us to stay in the same town—or county—once we grew up…and most of us didn't. And none of us dreamed of ever sleeping in the same room as adults that we'd spent our childhoods in. It's different here.

2

Halfway through our discussion of *A Separate Peace* in one of my junior classes, the door opened and all heads swung that way. Standing there, a rectangular slip of paper in her hand, was a very attractive, and *very* well-endowed brunette who looked totally out of place anywhere in Page County. She wore tight leather pants, a stretch top with some kind of sequined design, gold hoop earrings that a small monkey could have swung on, and a very stylishly designed hairdo. On her feet were leather shoes made out of some kind of animal skin, I was sure. And she was a real knockout. I could almost hear some of the guys suck in their breaths...and I could swear I heard some girls' nails grow two inches longer in a split second.

"Can I help you?" I asked.

"Yeah, I guess. You Mistah Finn?" she asked with a distinct New Yawk accent.

"Yes."

"Then heah," she said as she handed me the paper.

Glancing down, I realized it was a schedule form from guidance. "Maureen Denise Battaglia" it said. "*Battaglia*?! What's an Italian doing in Page County?" I thought. I doubt that you could find another Italian name in the whole phone book, at least not in the white pages.

"Hello. What's a nice Italian girl named Battaglia doin' way down here in Page County?" I asked with what I think was a smile.

"My fathah is buildin' that bunch o' townhouses an' that new ski resort. Believe me, I don't wanna be heah. Hey, you pronounced my name right! Every other hick in this school says the *g*!" she realized in some mild form of wonder.

I could hear the nails grow another inch when she'd said "hick."

I wrote her name on my roll and pointed to an empty seat toward the back, by the windows, telling her I'd get her her books at the end of class.

"Whatevah," she said, hoisting an equally expensive-looking purse up onto her shoulder, its swing making the purse miss a very important part of my anatomy by only about two inches.

Timmy, one of the boys in the front, noticed my quick move to avoid being castrated and starting laughing. She thought he was laughing at her.

"Somethin' funny?!" she snapped, looking down at him. "You laughin' at me?!"

That only got Timmy laughing harder. It looked as if she was going to say something else when Rachel, one of Ronnie's friends, interceded and said, "Don't mind him, he's partially brain-damaged," which got a few more laughing.

I put my hand on her shoulder and said, "Maureen, no one's laughing at you. Why don't you just go sit down, okay?"

She shrugged my hand away and, as she made her way to the seat, added, "An' don't call me Maureen…it's M.D."

That earned her a few more snickers. She sat there for the remaining ten minutes of class looking pissed-off and staring—or glaring—out the window and listening to nothing. I saw some of the girls sneaking peeks at her that I was surprised "M.D." couldn't feel penetrating her expensive top.

The bell rang, the kids filed out, and I got M.D. her books and told her where to find her next class.

"Is there anything to do in this rat hole or do they just drive tractors and eat cow crap?" she asked with a fake sweet smile.

"Where are you comin' from, M.D.?"

"You know how to say Italian names, you can't figger it out?"

"I'm from the Pittsburgh area and grew up with a lot of Italian kids…You, I'd guess Jersey or New York."

"Nawth Jersey...almost in New Yawk. You know wheah Pawk Ridge is?"

"No. Anywhere near Newark?"

She laughed derisively.

"Yeah, kinda, but far away enough that you can't smell it...or the people in it. Nevah mind. See you tomorrow, I guess." She sauntered out, leaving a trail of what I figured was expensive perfume hanging in the air. I wondered if the pants had been sprayed on.

"Hey, T, I hear you got the Slut of the North in your third-period class today," Ronnie whispered when she came into fifth.

"You need to tell Rachel to stop gossiping," I told her.

"What? No gossip? In Page County?! What are you, kiddin'?! It's the other religion!" Ronnie said, rolling her eyes. "Anyway, I ain'— *haven't* seen her yet but I hear she's somethin' else!"

"I'll let you decide, Slim," I whispered as more kids drifted in past us.

"Stop callin' me that, just 'cause I ain—*am not* built like your goddess, my sister!" she growled back in a whisper. "An' someone said she wants to be called 'M.D.' Is that right?"

"Yes, now go sit down and shuddup," I told her, holding my orange plastic bat as if I were going to swat her on her ass.

"M.D....what's that stand for, Mentally Deprived?!" Ronnie said with a giggle, ducking out of the way and going to her seat.

A similar conversation had taken place at lunch the period before. I'd just been taking my first bite of the coincidentally-enough Italian sausage sandwich I'd made for myself when Irene, her blond hair down for a change, sat down across from me in Ray's room, where the Lunch Bunch had been convening since right after the Christmas break.

"Whew, I got a new student in chem today and jeez, is she a pip!" Irene said in her husky voice.

"Lemme guess...M.D.?" I asked.
"You got her, too?"
"Yeah. Yeah, she's not exactly gonna fit in too well here, I don't think," I said with a laugh.
Wild Bill had just plopped himself and his Scooby Doo lunchbox down next to me.
"Who you talkin' about?" he asked, scratching at his scraggly beard.
"Fleas again? Or is it just the usual body lice?!" I asked him.
"Fuck you, Tommy Boy. So who you two talkin' about?"
"Just a new student Tom and I both got today...from Jersey, as a matter of fact. She's a bit of an asshole, too, Bill...too bad she's not special ed. You two could relate an' make her feel welcome," Irene chuckled sarcastically.
"Hey, you're from Jersey, too, Blondie!" Bill said but with his usual deranged smile.
"Yeah, but that's where the resemblance stops...between you and me *and* me and M.D."
"M.D.?! She goes by M.D.?"
"Yeah," I told him, "it's actually Maureen Denise Battaglia, but she wants to be call—"
"*Battaglia*?! The kid of the guy building the new ski resort over by Massanutten?!" Bill interrupted.
"Yeah, that's the one. She—"
"Holy shit, don't you two know anything?! Gerry Battaglia—her old man—he's connected, you morons. His old man's 'Big Rock' Battaglia. He owns half the garbage companies and most of the trucking companies in north Jersey and all around Atlantic City. He was A-One-major-mob-big-time when I was teachin' in Cape May. I read about Battaglia being the contractor for that new ski place but he doesn't really do any construction; he's just gotta be the money behind it. Betcha every single job up there is contracted out. They came down here 'cause there's no unions—at least ones they don't control—that they hafta deal with, I bet. Shit, the mob's in the county!" he said with a genuine laugh.

"Why didn't he put the daughter in private school? He's got the dough," I wondered half out loud.

"The only one around here's that Baptist one where they teach that Jerry Falwell is one step down from The Holy Ghost. No way a good Catholic father is gonna send his kid *there*," Irene observed.

"An' she sure wouldn't be able to dress like that, either," I added.

"You know, I wonder about that, now that Bill has told us who her old man is. Italian fathers—and especially ones involved in the mob—are usually pretty strict with their daughters an' want them to stay outta trouble and be low-keyed," Irene said.

"Maybe she's like some of the girls here—wears something else outta the house and then changes," I suggested.

"Umm, maybe," Irene said, turning to the taco that had been getting colder by the minute.

I was going to have a few illuminating experiences with M.D. before the year was over.

3

Less than a minute after the late bell rang for the fifth-period creative-writing class, another new student appeared at the door of 213. I knew who he was before I even looked at the slip in his hand. Dark, wavy hair, Mediterranean complexion, totally (again) out of place in northwestern Virginia—at least in *this* county—he could only be another Battaglia...and I wasn't wrong. But he was a lot different...a lot.

"Uhh, sorry I'm late. I kinda got lost on the way from lunch," he said softly, coming toward me with the slip held out.

"Ooh, he's cute!" I heard a girl whisper, and not too quietly.

The boy looked suitably embarrassed; he had heard the remark, too.

"Mark Dominick Battaglia," the name box told me. He was a senior.

"Hi. Guess I get both Battaglias, huh?" I said with a smile.

Like his sister, he looked a little startled when I'd pronounced the last name correctly; I guessed they were used to it being mispronounced. He also winced when I revealed that I had his sister.

"Yeah, sorry about that," he muttered with a shrug.

"I'm not...at least, not yet," I told him under my breath. "Welcome to the world of creative writing," I added, extending my hand.

He looked up and a smile forced its way across his face as he shook my hand. His handshake was firm and warm. He had that wavy, tight hair I always envied on the Italian friends of my boyhood; you know, the kind you can just run your fingers through and everything just lies there, neat and in place. Dark brown eyes that smiled, a very handsome young face; the eyes were penetrating and I liked him immediately. I tend to like anyone who will look right back into my eyes, especially with eyes that seem to smile.

I pointed out the seat behind Ronnie; I thought she was going to have a stroke. Her mouth opened, closed, opened again; the girl to her left, Laura, her "best best friend," as she had told me repeatedly, waved a hand in front of Ronnie's face as if Ronnie were going to faint. Fortunately (for them), Mark hadn't turned around again after he had turned back to look at me.

"I assume you go by Mark?" I asked.

"Yeah, no dumb initials. My mom thought it was cute to give us both names with the same initials; my sister doesn't think so but she uses them anyway. Go figure."

"What about you?"

He shrugged. "A name's a name, isn't it?" he said and then turned to take his seat.

I'd noticed something else about the brother: he didn't have as much of a pronounced Jersey accent as M.D.

As in third period, the girls couldn't keep their eyes off the Battaglia kid, but the looks were the total opposite of the ones M.D. had received. And instead of nails, I swore I could hear hearts beating and salivary glands becoming active. The handful of boys in the class looked unaffected and relatively disinterested in the whole thing, although I did notice Jimmie Campbell nod and smile when Mark had sat down to his right.

"Okay, ladies and germs, you folks are gonna start writing up your commercials for the videos you're gonna make," I began and then started telling them what the guidelines were and what they had to do.

The rest of the period flew by once the questioning ended and I let them get started. I noticed that Jimmie and his girlfriend-of-the-moment Kristi had invited Mark to work on a commercial with them;

I'd watched as he gave them the same nonchalant shrug, a smile, and then had clustered with them in the back corner. Ronnie had looked somewhat disappointed that she and Laura hadn't gotten to him first.

When the bell rang, I caught Mark's eye and waved him to me.

"Here's the textbook. You need to have a notebook with you every day, a small spiral notebook for your daybook, and daily access to a computer with an up-to-date word-processing program on it. Any problem there?"

"Naah, I just hooked mine up Saturday. Microsoft Word okay?" he asked.

"Yeah, perfect; all the computers in the school have that, including the writing lab where we'll be working every week. Gotta be a little rough on you to move in your senior year, so close to graduating," I added.

He shrugged and shook his head.

"Not really. I was in a prep school back in Jersey an' I hated it…and the guys in it. All spoiled little turds with their Lexuses and BMW's. I never heard so much whining in my life. I wanted my dad to let me go to public school, but, well….everyone knows our family up there…or at least our name, an'….anyway."

"Next year?" I asked.

"I got applications in to William and Mary, Georgetown, Emory, Princeton, and a few others."

"Know what you wanna do?"

"I think, at least for now, I wanna go into law…maybe immigration stuff," he told me with another shrug.

"How're your grades and SAT's…if I'm not bein' too nosy," I added.

Another shrug.

"Last time my mom checked, the G.P.A. was 4.3-something 'cause I've taken all these advanced classes…and I got a 1490 on the SAT's an' over 600 on the SAT II's that I've taken. I think I've got a good chance at those colleges."

"Yeah, I'd say so!" I remarked, impressed.

"An' listen, Mr. Finn…don't compare me to my dumbass sister, *please*! I swear she was either dropped on her head at birth or she had the UPS man for a father…an' Jesus, don't tell my parents I ever said that. Damn, I shouldn'ta said that!"

"It's all right, my lips are sealed," I told him with a pat on the shoulder, which I noticed was firm and muscular. "You better get to sixth period. Lemme write you a pass."

When I got home that afternoon, Sandi was just getting out of the Mustang, a brown Food Lion bag in her hand.

"What's in the bag, babe?" I asked in my best seductive voice.

"Dinner. I know what I was feeling like, so I got the stuff to make it on the way home," she replied, giving me a hot, wet kiss and smacking me in the back with the damn bag.

"Ouch! What the hell you got in there?!" I grumbled.

"Horseshit and splinters, your favorite!" she said, dashing ahead toward the front door with a laugh as I made to smack her ass.

Half an hour later, she was cutting up the fresh mushrooms for the beef stroganoff while I cubed the nicely marbled piece of London broil she had picked out, beginning to brown it in the olive oil.

"Stop with the mushrooms; do the onions next," I told her.

"Yes, *sir*!" she said with a salute, managing to launch a slice of the fungus that had stuck to the knife into the air where it decided to keep going until it had stuck to the low ceiling.

"Great! *You* can get that off!" I muttered.

"Yeah, I will, an' I'll slip it onto your plate when you're not looking if you don't smile. What's bugging *you* tonight, anyway?"

I hadn't really been aware of being in a bad mood or anything until she'd said that; then I realized I had brought home the grumpies because of something that had occurred at the end of the day

4

There's this female teacher in my department; her name is Miss Dunbar. She has been at Mountain Valley High for over twenty years and she is crazy. Maybe crazy isn't the most accurate word; I think *psychotic* with a pinch of *hallucinatory* might be the operative terms. Okay, let's be accurate: she's nuts.

You see, she has this tendency to be in the middle of teaching something—when she *does* make the attempt to actually teach—and she will suddenly get this somewhat dazed look on her rather gaunt face, look straight ahead or up at the ceiling, and begin talking to someone who's not there. Sometimes it appears to be her mother; other times, it's what people have figured out is a twin sister or a dead brother. I know, because since late September, I have been getting new students—a total of eleven as of three o'clock this afternoon—students who were originally assigned to Dunbar but who were so freaked out when she would go off into La-La-land that their parents insisted that their children have another teacher, which is why my two accelerated junior English classes are now at the state maximum enrollment number of thirty; Ray has also gotten four of her escapees.

"Hey, what's the story on Mabel Dunbar?" Ray had asked back in early October when we'd both gotten a couple refugees each. We were sitting on my little back porch with a couple beers.

"I don't know. Why don't you ask Judi Clapton? She seems to know everything historical around here."

"I don' know. I hate to look like I'm joining in on the gossip culture."

"Just bring the subject of Mabel up sometime when you're having a mentor meeting with Judi about English or somethin'," I suggested. About a week or so later, we were shoving down sandwiches during our twenty-two-minute lunch "hour" when Ray filled us in.

"Well, supposedly, she has a twin sister named Clara and a brother who died in Korea named Michael. She talks to them. She hates Clara because supposedly Mom liked Clara better than Mabel, and she has made the brother some kind of heroic god who would have saved her from the angst of the Dunbar family if he hadn't joined the Marines and gotten killed."

"How does anyone know all this stuff?" Irene and Deb, our computer genius, had asked together.

"Evidently she's been doin' this nutso stuff for years and all the veteran teachers know about it. It's supposed to be a big joke among the faculty," Ray said with a shrug.

"It's not a big joke to a couple of the girls I've inherited from her," I told them. "One of my girls, Susan, got so freaked out when Dunbar'd go off that her doctor had to prescribe some kind of medication for her. She's off it now, since they transferred her to me in November."

"Well, if the faculty know about it, it musta gotten back to the administration and Paul," Deb observed. Paul Morgan is the head of the English department, by the way.

"It has and it did, but Judi said the two previous principals didn't want to touch the whole thing 'cause Mabel's tenured and it would take a shitload of documentation and court time to prove she's incapable of fulfilling her contractual duties or somethin' like that, an' when Don got here four years ago, someone told him that the Dunbars have been in the county forever and have a couple influential friends on the board of supervisors *and* the school board, so he needed to look the other way as a new principal an' not make waves an' just hope Mabel retires soon," Ray informed us.

"Boy, ol' Claptrap has her ears to the information pipeline," Wild Bill mumbled through his egg-salad sandwich that was busy dropping itself all over the piece of plastic wrap it had come to school in.

"Bill, the egg bits don't look too good in the beard," Irene whispered loudly over her bowl of microwaved soup.
I saw Mabel in action about a week later.

I was walking down the first-floor hall on my way to the library when I heard her high-pitched voice coming out of her room.
"...oh, no, *Mabel* can't go to the dance because there is only one dress and *Clara* must wear it....*Mabel* has to stay home and clean the bathroom...I will *not* help her with her speech, Mother!...Why did Father have to leave, Mother?!...I....I...I will not..."
As I passed, I risked a glance into the room; the students that I could see, about a half dozen scattered across the front, were staring wide-eyed, their mouths hanging open, except for one redneck kid with the Dale Earnhardt hat who was laughing silently and looking back at someone else in the room.
Mabel Dunbar was staring straight ahead, as though she were standing in front of what I guessed was a vision of her mother. Her left hand held an open paperback, the arm hanging down against her hip; her right hand was clutching her long, bony throat. It was more than a little freaky. As I felt myself walk faster, I suddenly knew what the students trapped in those classes with her must have felt.

"I thought I must've told you about Miss Dunbar," Sandi said as we started in on the stroganoff...after I had apologized about the mood and had explained. "An' you never mentioned anything about getting her kids transferring into your classes."
"Guess I had more important things on my mind the first half of the year...you know, learning to teach, the Knopf thing, this blond sex kitten who was sucking the breath out of me every time I was near her...you know, dumb stuff like that."
"Yeah, ha-ha...anyway, I remember the kids who had her talkin' about her and the invisible people in the room...I'm just glad I never had her. I had Mrs. Walker for freshman English—she retired two

years ago—an' then Mr. Kramer for sophomore, an'…oh, yeah, Miss Schick when I was a junior—she's gone, too—and of course, you know who I had my senior year."

"Anyway, I'm sorry I was grumpy. At least I can't get any *more* students now."

That evening, after I'd finished grading one batch of essays, we sat in front of the fire that was popping and crackling in the stone fireplace, Sandi leaning against me in my Penguins jersey again. She seemed to have become very attached to it, as a matter of fact, not that I minded. She looked a lot better in it than I'm sure I did, and she looked a lot better in it than any Pittsburgh Penguins hockey player would, and knowing that there was nothing under it but her did a lot for me.

"Talk to me," she whispered.

"Whaddaya want me to talk about?"

"I don't care. I just like listening to your voice. I love that gravelly voice, almost like a wildcat's purr. I feel so safe when you talk, when you hold me. An' you're so damn passionate about everything. Is there anything you don't get passionate about?" she asked, nuzzling her blond head against my cheek and shoulder.

"Yeah, sure."

"Like what?"

"Asparagus…damp towels…snot—ouch! Dammit!"

"Be serious!"

"I don't know…never thought about it before. What am I supposed to be so passionate about…other than you?" I wanted to know.

"Teaching…your kids…us…cooking…pizza an' beer, for God's sake…the way you make love to me, sometimes soft, sometimes like you're trying to devour me…"

"I am. I want to roll you into a little ball and just eat you all up," I said.

"Well, you do *some* of that…anyway…an' even when you tell

stories…like about your childhood, or Pop, or your mom…funny stuff, serious stuff…the Air Force stuff…"

"Well, I guess if you don't have passion in your life, your life's pretty dull and lifeless; don't you agree?"

"Yeah, but the passion was all dried up an' gone in my life until last summer, sweetie…now, I can't get enough of it, but it scares me, too," she said, surprising me.

"What're you scared about?!"

"Losin' you, havin' this end. I want to feel you, touch you, absorb you until you've become a part of me…but if I ever lost you, I know I wouldn't be able to exist. Tom, I've *never* felt like this…I never thought it was possible to feel anything like this," she said, pushing away from me and looking up into my eyes with blue eyes of her own…eyes that had begun to fill.

"Oh, shit, don't! Stop! I'm not going anywhere. I love you, you stupid blond thing. You know what Tina, one of my best kids, told me today? She said I was glowing. *You* make me glow…you make the blood race through my body. All you have to do is appear and my goddam heart either stops and starts beating like a…a…shit, I don't know. Look, I'm here an' I'm not going anywhere. Don't you think I have the same fear—that this'll all get old and you'll decide I was better than the asshole you had before me but—"

She pushed her fingers against my lips and pushed me back, crawling on top of me and smothering me with kisses while the tears trapped in her eyes dropped onto my own cheeks.

I made love to her gently…with passion, but gently…that night…but she chose to try to devour me.

5

"Hey, Mr. F., we gonna be able to get into the writing lab this week?" Bob asked as he came into fifth period a week later on Tuesday.

"Yeah, I have us scheduled for Thursday an' Friday. Don't you ever listen to anything I say?" I growled.

"When did you say that?" he asked with the usual quizzical expression on his thin face as he pushed his glasses back up to the bridge of his nose.

"Probably when you weren't paying attention...duh! Anyway, why?"

"Well, I got this really great idea for my commercial an' the computer at home is at the shop gettin' re-configurated or somethin' so I have to do all my work in school, an' I got this really great idea for my commercial last night an' chucked the other idea, so now I have to do all my work in school, an'—"

"An' you got this really great idea for a commercial and you wanna get working on it, right?" I asked.

"Yeah, how'd you know?" he asked.

"Just psychic, I guess."

"What's psychology got to do with it?" Bob asked with another confused look.

Fortunately, some other kids were waiting to talk to me before class began, so Bob had to spare me another variation on the same theme.

The creative-writing class—now minus Crystal, now containing Mark—had become my favorite bunch of kids, followed closely by the Period 3 junior class. Don't get me wrong, I like all my kids, with the exception of a few whiners and slackers, but some classes just come together and instead of a group of individuals, they become almost like a family...and yeah, sometimes with the kinds of squabbles that occur in a family.

Like the time, right after Christmas vacation, when the kids had gotten the news about Sandi and me and had thrown a surprise party for us. Well, a surprise for me, since when she walked into my classroom that period on that day, everyone had known why she was there but me.

Ronnie had been behind it all, of course. They'd bought us two presents: a wedding album to be filled in, and a double picture frame made up of two intersecting silver hearts. It didn't take much to deduce that some of the girls had been the ones who'd picked out the presents; the guys would've gotten us a six-pack and a case of car wax or motor oil.

Anyway, there'd been a ton of cookies, mostly chocolate chip, that the girls and/or their moms had baked, and it had been impossible, even with the kids with appetites like piranhas, for them all to be finished that day, so I'd taken the rest home, picked up a large cookie tin from the local dollar store, and had brought them back the following Monday for kids to nibble when they needed a sugar rush.

Well, one afternoon, Danny had opened the lid of the tin to find only a thousand crumbs and three cookie bits, all in the shape of rounded triangles.

"Hey, who left all these bits in here?! An' who ate all the cookies?!" he shouted, startling those of us who hadn't been expecting anyone to be yelling.

"What's the matter?" I asked.

Danny stood there, holding the bottom part of the tin toward me.

"Lookit this! Last time I went for a cookie there musta been at least three dozen in here! Who the h—...who ate 'em all?! Whadda we got, a pig in here?!"

Well, by this time, most of the kids had arrived for class and were all clustered around Danny.

"I didn't."

"Not me."

"I'm on a diet!"

"Man, nothin' but a bunch o' crumbs!"

After getting them seated and calmed down, I addressed...or tried to address...the "problem."

"So okay, look, it's no big deal...so who ate them all? I don't remember seeing anyone devouring thirty or forty cookies...does anyone?"

Well, after a half-minute of people who weren't guilty trying desperately *not* to look guilty, and going on trust, we pretty much agreed that none of them had eaten that many cookies that fast, or that frequently.

"Well, if it wasn't any of us, it musta been kids in some of your other classes," Ronnie suggested.

I shook my head.

"Nope, I only take this out for you kids and I put this tin under my desk after fifth period."

There was a brief silence as they either stared at me, the ceiling, or at one another.

"I got it. Let's buy some more cookies, put 'em in the tin, and Donny and me'll rig up the video camera from the Media One kids, the one with the motion trigger thing on it," Jimmie suggested.

"That should've been Donny and *I*...where you gonna put the camera, bright boy?" I asked.

"Can't we stick it in between those books back there?" Donny, who I had dubbed "Mystery Man" (but that's another story) asked, pointing to the bookcase in the back of the room.

"Well, you figure out how to conceal it, you figure out how to rig it up, and you figure out how to swear this class full of talkative idiots to secrecy in a county that thrives on gossip, and you're on," I told him.

Well, they did. The camera worked all right, they managed to conceal it, leaving only the lens exposed, and with my assurance that if we found out who had talked—if someone did—that person would flunk the class and get a referral so terrible that they wouldn't be allowed to go to the prom…they put their plan into action.

I bought four bags of generic chocolate chip cookies at Food Lion; Donny suggested dipping some of them in dog piss but that got voted down; another suggestion that we buy and melt some Ex-Lax and dip some in that was also nixed by yours truly.

"But we'll know who it is 'cause he'll be runnin' to the john all the time—"

"Or crappin' in his pants every ten minutes!" said Ronnie.

"How you know it's a guy, Ronnie? Maybe it's one o' those fat girls who looks like a water buffalo," John argued.

"Yeah, guys ain't—*aren't* the only pigs in this school!" Eric added.

"It doesn't matter—we are *not* doing anything with Ex-Lax!" I shouted, shutting them all up, once I gave them all The Look. Actually, I kind of enjoyed it as I watched Ronnie trying to slide down in her seat to hide until she was below desk level.

We put the cookies in the tin, slid it to where I always put it under my desk, and waited.

On his way out of class that day, Mark Battaglia, who had pretty much sat back, finding the whole thing somewhat silly, whispered, "Maybe Donny and Jimmie have futures with my grandfather and dad," and with a wink, left.

The mystery was pretty much anti-climactic; it was over almost before the suspense could even begin to build.

6

I'd just unlocked the door to 213 the following morning when I looked to see Donny and Jimmie coming down the hall.

"You guys are early," I observed.

"Gotta check the camera!" Donny said, hurriedly brushing past me, Jimmie at his heels.

A minute or so later, in the tiny screen on the camcorder, the three of us were watching Hollins Johnson, the janitor assigned to the second floor, coming into view. He went right to my desk, sat down in the chair, rolled it back, ducked down and emerged with the cookie tin. Looking furtively toward the door, he opened the tin. We watched—Jimmie and Donny laughed, actually—as his eyes got very wide in his dark face as he discovered the new load of cheap cookies.

With the deft speed of the stage magician, he somehow managed to shove three into his mouth, stuffed a whole handful into his overalls' pocket as he stood up, then put the tin back where it had been.

"Man, he's so skinny! How can he eat like that an' still look like a stork?!" Jimmie exclaimed.

"He's a damn thief," Donny grumbled.

"Oh, give me a break, Donny, they're only cookies, an' Food Lion brand on top of that," I told him.

"Yeah, maybe so, but who knows what else he's swiped in the past. He doesn't look like—hey, *now* look, Mr. F.!"

As we watched, Hollins gave another quick glance in the direction of the door and then tugged on the long top drawer of my desk.

"See? He's tryin' to get into your desk!" Donny proclaimed triumphantly.

"Hmm...glad I bought a new lock at the hardware store over Christmas," I muttered. "Maybe you're right. A laser pointer an' my hand-held tape recorder mysteriously disappeared from that drawer back in the fall. Maybe I need to have a little talk with Hollins."

"Why talk to him?! Just report him to the head custodian, Mr. Jeck, an' get his ass fired!" Donny said.

"Jeck?!" Jimmie said with a laugh. "The guy's weird, man! Last year, one of my teachers sent me to ask him for a new sponge to clean his board with an' Jeck told me that sponges were illegal an' students couldn't have them!"

"I'll take care of it, Donny, just relax," I interrupted. "And listen, you two, you don't tell anyone about this other than that we solved the mystery."

"But they're all gonna wanna know who the cookie thief is!" Jimmie argued.

"Yeah, I know. Well, we'll just tell 'em that we don't want the person to get into any major trouble an' that it's not gonna happen again. That's gonna hafta satisfy them, 'cause the whole school'll know about it if it doesn't stop right here with the three of us," I told them.

"Yeah, but remember that Ben Franklin quote you put on the board one day: 'Three can keep a secret if two of them are dead'?" Jimmie reminded me.

"Yeah, well, then I'm just gonna hafta kill you two, I guess...now shut up. Gimme that tape an' take the camera back to Chuck when school starts," I said.

That afternoon, I left my room, locking the door. I went down to the library, returned a couple books I'd borrowed, giving Hollins Johnson enough time to get to my room. Sure enough, he was just entering when I came through the doors at the end of the hall. He was just sitting down in my chair when I walked in.

If guilt can be painted across a person's face, then Hollins was wearing a mural. The whites of his eyes were so exposed that I wouldn't have been surprised to see his eyeballs pop right out and roll across the desk.

"Before you snack on the cookies, Hollins," I said, closing the door behind me, "we need to have a little talk."

To Hollins' credit, he didn't try to lie, but he struggled a little when I raised the issue of the two items that had been stolen back over Thanksgiving break. I could almost read his mind as it contemplated the difference between stealing some cookies, as compared to a laser pointer and a tape recorder. I decided to try to make it easier for him.

"Hollins, if a certain laser pointer and a Sony cassette recorder happen to show up on my desk, like tomorrow morning before I get here, I think we can agree that Hollins Johnson's days of borrowing what's not his are over. If you can't agree with that, well, the videotape that's in that desk drawer you tried so hard to get into yesterday, the video that you're the star of, well, Mr. Jeck and Mr. Dempsey are gonna hafta see it an' Hollins Johnson's going to have to start practicing to say 'Paper or plastic' or 'You want fries with that?'…you understand, Hollins?"

His Adam's apple must've bobbed up and down ten times as he swallowed very rapidly, stood up, and left. I could almost see a tiny trail of dustballs caught up in the airy vortex of his departure.

A laser pointer and the recorder were sitting on the desk when I got there the next day. I wondered if Hollins had just kept speeding all the way home the previous afternoon to get them…or if he'd had them in some locker or stashed somewhere else in the school. Anyway, they were back. I wasn't sure whether I should erase the videotape or not, in case Hollins' conversion was only temporary; I locked it, unerased, in the closet in my room, the one that had also stored a .32 Beretta very temporarily earlier that year.

A couple weeks passed with nothing notable happening. I was beginning to enjoy Mark Battaglia's still-quiet presence in my class;

his sister was another story, however.

It became very obvious, very quickly—to everyone—that M.D. was a very unhappy kid. There wasn't a day since she'd arrived that I'd seen her smile, or even come close to one. Neither had any of the other teachers I knew who had her. In addition, she'd had two referrals written on her by lunch monitors for refusing to return her dirty tray in the cafeteria and had already had one parent conference for disrespect, prior to a one-day, in-school suspension. That had been because of something that had happened in Deb's computer-science class.

"All I asked her to do was throw away the scrap paper that she'd left at her computer station," Deb explained at lunch one day.

"Whaddid she say?" Wild Bill asked, fighting with a stringy piece of ham that finally flew out from his sandwich and stuck to the front of his shirt. "Shit!"

"She told me she wasn't 'an effing maid' and told me that's what we have janitors for," Deb explained, trying to keep from laughing as she watched Bill smearing a little dab of mustard into a wider stain. "First referral I've ever had to write. I didn't want to, but all the other kids were listening, an' I couldn't just let it go, right?"

We all nodded.

"What's the mother like?" Irene asked, brushing some of her burnished blond hair back over an ear.

"Oh, she was so embarrassed that I felt sorry for her. She just kept apologizing. Meanwhile, M.D. kept making these sighing sounds; I could almost *hear* her thinking how ridiculous the whole thing was. She really strikes me as spoiled rotten."

"Maybe M.D. oughta stand for Major Dysfunction," Ray suggested.

"Well, I could tell that Mrs. Battaglia didn't want to acknowledge that it stood for *My Daughter*. She just looked like she wanted to go somewhere and hide," Deb added.

"Y' know," I interjected, "usually, kids whose parents—or at least fathers—are connected like Battaglia is, if Bill's right about his connections—"

"Hey, when have I ever been wrong?!" Bill said, stopping his dabbing at the mustard stain with a now-water-wet napkin. Meanwhile, the rest of us fought back the urge to laugh in response to his question.

"Anyway, those kinds of parents usually insist that their children be very respectful and not make any kind of waves. Even just plain Italian families…at least the ones I know and grew up around," I said.

"I think she's just rebelling against her father," Irene said. "Maybe she's really embarrassed about where his money comes from."

"Or maybe she thinks she oughta be spoiled even more…and she sure as hell doesn't wanna be here, in the middle of cow-patty country!" Ray insisted.

"An' what about the outfits she wears? I saw enough cleavage in the past few weeks that I could build a tunnel!" I said.

"So, Tom, what are *you* lookin' at?" Irene asked with a twinkle in her blue eyes.

"Come on, Irene, with boobs like that, they're kinda hard to ignore," I replied with a shrug. "Actually, I wish she'd cover 'em up so I can get all the guys in third period to pay attention to *me*…and the girls all wanna set fire to her, I think."

"Good luck, sweetie," Irene said, standing up and deftly tossing her balled-up lunch bag into the garbage can on the other side of the room.

"Where'd you learn to shoot like that?" Wild Bill asked.

"Volleyball," Irene said with a laugh as she left.

"*Volleyball*?!" Bill asked with a look of total confusion on his hairy face.

That wouldn't be the last conversation among the Lunch Bunch with M.D. for the subject.

When I got back to our cabin that afternoon, I was more than a little surprised to find a huge load of split oak and hickory stacked neatly against the wall of the small front porch.

7

"Hey, Mom," I asked Becky, my now-step-mother and stood-to-be mother-in-law, "you know anything about that big load of wood at the cabin?" when I walked into the motel office.

Becky looked up from the checkbook she'd been writing in and brushed a strand of gray hair off her cheek.

"Some black man brought it by around nine this morning in an old pickup that smoked so much I thought it was a crop duster," she said.

"What did he look like?"

"Black! That's all. Jeans, old Army jacket, rusty ol' pickup with built-up sides made o' plywood."

"Was he kinda skinny?" I asked.

"Skinny?! He looked like a damn stick! I couldn't believe he could lift any o' that firewood. How come you felt like you hadda buy wood? Don't I supply you with enough?" she asked with a quizzical look.

"I didn't buy anything…but I think I know why I got it."

Hollins was making sure I wouldn't do anything with the videotape. I erased it the next morning. When I left that afternoon, I left a thank-you note on my desk, telling him that I didn't need any more wood; the note was gone when I got to school the next morning. By the way, it was really good, well-seasoned wood.

That night, I'd had a pot of pasta amatriciana waiting on the stove by the time Sandi got home from her late class.

"Ummm, what's that smell?" she'd called from the little living room as she was taking off her ski jacket.

"Pasta amatriciana, somethin' new," I called back. "Pat Conroy wrote about it in *Beach Music,* so I looked it up on the Internet and we get to see if it's any good."

"If you made it an' it's Italian, it's gonna be good, sweet man," she said, coming into the kitchen to hug me from behind. "What's in it?"

"It's basically a marinara sauce but the extra ingredient is bacon…or pancetta, but that's kinda hard to find around here," I replied.

"What's pancetta?"

"Like Italian bacon, but not quite the same. This'll be okay with bacon."

"Sounds sorta like a BLT with pasta," she observed. I grunted.

"Have a good day?" she asked to begin our usual opening conversation.

"Yeah, sure. See the wood on the porch, by the way?" I asked.

"No, I didn't notice," she said, going back into the front of the cabin and opening to front door and turning on the light. It was still a month before daylight-saving time and dark by the time she got home from that four o'clock class. "Hey, where'd *that* come from?" she asked as she came back into the kitchen.

I told her.

"Mr. Johnson was there when I was in school. We always used to say he looked like a black Bic pen with a black Nerf ball on top."

"Yeah, well, your mom said he looks like a stick. He still looks the same, although I guess his hair's shorter now."

"Well, when I was there, he was the only black guy who still had an Afro. Even the few black guys I knew used to laugh at him and that bush!" Sandi told me. "An' when is that pasta gonna be done?! It smells so good I wanna stick my head in the pot…plus I'm starvin'. I didn't eat anything all day!"

"Don't you go gettin' skinny on me!" I growled. "You lose one ounce off that ass or those boobs an' it's over between us."

"Oh, so now you're tellin' me it's just T-and-A that makes you want me?" she asked with a pout.

"Only in that other room there, the one with the bed and the pig called Mary; the rest of the time I'll love you for your brains...except when we're doing it on the floor, or in the shower, the couch, or—*ouch*! Goddamit, that hurt!" I groaned, rubbing my ribs.

"Serves you right!" she said, opening the small refrigerator and handing me a Rolling Rock. "Here, drink this and shut up before you say anything else that might incriminate you. Aren't you gonna ask me how *my* day was?" she asked, plopping herself down in a kitchen chair.

"So...how was *your* day, *dear*?" I asked deliberately.

"Oh, I thought you'd never ask. Let's see...got an A on the last paper in the wilderness lit. class...got approved to do my student teaching next fall...an' oh, yeah, Mountain Valley High's the place. Nothing much else."

It took me a couple seconds.

"Mountain Valley? You're gonna be student teaching *here* next year?!"

"Yup!" she said, jumping up and hugging me. "We'll almost be, like, colleagues."

"Mister and Missus Finn, colleagues. Cool, as Ronnie would say!"

She backed away momentarily, looking down at her left hand and my mother's engagement ring.

"You're still sure about July?" she asked hesitantly.

"What the hell are you askin' that for? I'd marry you today if Pop and Becky didn't insist on a church thing! You know that!"

"You know, I've been thinkin' about that a lot lately," she said, sitting back down. "Look, we don't go to church, so why have it in a church? I'd rather just have a simple ceremony. The commissioner of marriages can come out here and we can do it outside, like just with some roses or somethin'. It feels so hypocritical to do the whole church thing...plus the one Mom talked about having it in is filled with all those fake Baptists who think they're the only true Christians an' talk about everyone else. Really, Tom, the more I think about it, the less I wanna do it that way."

"Commissioner of marriages?"

"Is that all you can say? Yeah, there's some guy who gets paid to be the commissioner of marriages for the county," she explained. "Don't they have someone like that back in Pennsylvania?"

"No. Just judges and I think they still have justices-of-the-peace...which always made me laugh," I told her.

"Whaddaya mean?"

"You know, justice-of-the-*peace*...it almost implies that he had to make *peace* between the two people before he could marry them!" Sandi laughed.

"Yeah, an' what about the marriages that didn't wind up havin' a lot of peace in them an' were more like wars?" she asked.

"Then I guess they should give refunds," I said, laughing as well. When I stopped and the tension in the discussion was gone, I told her that we could talk about changing our plans.

"But if we're gonna do that, why wait till July?" I asked.

"No reason to. But I wanna get married when it's nice an' warmer, so maybe late April or May?"

"Yeah, okay. That way, we can go straight from the ceremony to the woods up on the mountain and consummate the marriage, naked, in the forest...totally natural for a totally natural act between two people in love," I suggested facetiously.

"Oooh, I like that!" she murmured.

"Now all we have to do is get Becky and Pop to agree," I reminded her.

"Umm...can we eat now?" she reminded me back.

"You *are* referring to the pasta, right?" I asked. "I mean, with all this sex talk, I—okay, okay, I'm getting it!"

The pasta turned out great; we had dessert in that other room.

That same week, it was time for the kids in my creative-writing class to film their commercials. I'd reserved the studio that the Media One kids and Chuck Hoffman used to broadcast the morning announcements from; I'd also reserved Chuck and two of his best kids to help me with my limited video knowledge and skills.

The studio, small but well equipped with top-of-the-line video stuff, was housed at the back of the new library addition in the rear of Mountain Valley High. While we were filming the individual commercials, the rest of the class was out in the library, practicing and rehearsing, much to the dismay of the two librarians, Miss Klempf and Mrs. Gaucher. I had told my students, repeatedly and firmly, to be more than necessarily respectful and quiet. On numerous occasions in the past year, I had noticed that when more than a dozen students are in the library and anywhere near Miss Klempf, she starts to shake and her voice becomes a quavering gurgle.

Most of the kids' commercials were predictably juvenile, but still funny for the most part; three moments in the filming, however, will stay in my memory forever.

8

The commercials attempted to sell everything from used cars to cooking utensils and appliances to detergents, most parodying those that we'd all seen on television. I guess my favorite from the prescription-drug category was the one that David, Shawna, and Debbie did for a drug designed to get rid of stress.

As the commercial opened, again convincing me that Dave was destined for bigger and better things on the West Coast, Debbie, a stunning redhead, was looking at the camera, wearing a melancholy expression on her face. Then Shawna, a short girl with dark-blonde hair, approached, asking, "Hey, Deb, what's the matter?"

"Stress is killing me! I think I'll just kill myself first an' get it over with!" Debbie groaned melodramatically.

"Stress? From what?" Shawna asked, in an equally over-melodramatic tone.

"Oh, God. First, I have Mrs. Quackenbush's algebra test today, I have a tennis match this afternoon and my tendonitis is acting up, my mom and dad are getting a divorce because my mom has become a lesbian, I have seventeen essays to write for Mr. Finn's *stupid* creative-writing class, I have to work an extra fifty hours tonight at Wal-Mart, I still haven't sent out any college applications, my feet are killin' me, I think I have earwax build-up, my boyfriend just told me he's gonna try bein' gay, my cat's pregnant again, and I have to pee real bad!"

"Well, Deb, you really need to do what I did!" Shawna said sympathetically.

"What *you* did? What did *you* do?" Deb asked with a horribly confused expression.

45

"I got Stress-B-Gone tablets, and there's no more stress in my life!" Shawna proclaimed proudly, holding up a small box about the size of the typical aspirin box on which they'd glued a computer-printed "Stress-B-Gone."

Then they'd stopped the tape, replacing the background of the studio wall with Dave, who was now in front of the open window so that there was nothing behind him but the woods outside the back of the school. And there, in a white medical smock, grinning into the camera, wearing a pair of old black-framed glasses, complete with adhesive tape between the lenses, and with one tooth blackened out with black electrical tape, was Dave, holding up the same box.

"Yes, that's right, folks. Just get yourself some Stress-B-Gone and life will be stress-free forever!" Then they stopped the tape again to allow Dave to get out from in front of the camera, which then began taping again. As the camera zoomed in on nothing but the woods, we could hear Dave's voice say,

"Users of Stress-B-Gone may experience some slight, minor side effects such as itching, nostril dandruff, deafness, nosebleed, unexpected pregnancy, inability to breathe, high fever, coughing, impotence, hives, sudden sexual desire for farm animals, warts, complete loss of bladder control, glowing, deprivation of air, sleeplessness, bleeding gums, nose drip, earwax buildup, swollen joints, beer joints, beer nuts, impotence, nymphomania, baptism, loss of limbs, rigor mortis, habeas corpus, singing like Michael Bolton, weightlessness, Carpathian syndrome, vampirism, addiction to disco music, leprosy, radioactivity, speaking in tongues, spontaneous combustion, and possible death."

And they did it all in one take. Once I got Chuck and his two camera people's hysterics under control, we did Ronnie's commercial for hamster hash.

Then there was the one by John and Eric, and a strange kid named Dan they had borrowed from Irene's fifth-period chemistry class.

What the viewer saw in this commercial were three guys in

undershirts and boxer shorts, the middle one holding a small bush that had wet dirt clinging to the rootball. The one on the left was Eric, a thin, curly-haired kid with a sloping nose and crossed eyes; the one on the right was John, a tall, round fellow who just always looked jolly; the one in the middle was this dark-haired kid named Dan that I didn't know, in Clark Kent glasses. They all wore Santa Claus hats...don't ask me why.

The one in the middle, Dan, looking at the camera, spoke.

"Hi, there, folks. Need something to make your property look better?"

"Yeah, wanna plant some cool stuff around the house?" Eric chimed in, still with his eyes crossed.

"Yup, yup, yup, plant something nice, plant something nice!" John said in what was supposed to be a somewhat retarded or moronic voice.

"Well...." Dan began, and then, with no musical accompaniment, they began singing...and singing horribly:

> When you want to plant a tree,
> When you want something to see,
> Call the Nursery Boys today,
> We'll come running, right away,
> We'll plant you a tree,
> Or plant you a bush,
> But ya better pay us or we'll kick your tush!

Then they danced and hopped around in a circle, shaking the bush, which was dropping dirt all over the floor. Well, it was supposed to be dancing, but they looked more like crazed worshipers of some strange religion who were suffering from severe cases of jock itch, chanting "Nursery Boys!" over and over again until they disappeared from the screen.

It wouldn't be until the end of that school year that I'd find out what was really behind that commercial.

And then there was Bob. Remember Bob?

"Well, I got this really great idea for my commercial an' the computer at home is at the shop gettin' re-configurated or somethin' so I have to do all my work in school, an' I got this really great idea for my commercial last night an' chucked the other idea, so now I have to do all my work in school, an'—"

Yeah, *that* Bob.

We were all set to film Bob, and Chuck went over the same instructions he'd given the other kids.

"Okay, Bob, ya see the two cameras? The one Karen is manning will be the one that shoots close-ups of just your face; the one Andy is behind will do long shots and zoom in and out. You look at the one that has the red light on; if you see the red light go out, turn to face the other one. Got it?"

Bob, wearing an Atlanta Braves cap, a plaid shirt and jeans, nodded eagerly, while he held a grocery bag that contained something. Chuck and I left the part of the studio with the cameras and closed the door to the tiny control booth where Jimmie, who'd taken Media One the year before, was working the toggle switches that controlled which of the cameras was "live." Wearing a headset, he communicated with the two camera operators who also wore headsets, telling them when their cameras were going to be "taking tape." In front of him was a wall of tiny camera screens, nine of them. Chuck stood behind him, while I stood to the side, trying to stay out of everyone's way, which was not too easy in the approximately eight-by-eight cubicle.

"Okay, Karen, gonna start with you," Jimmie said; then, throwing another switch which activated the speakers in the filming room, said, "Okay, Bob, can you hear me?"

As I looked at the two tiny television screens that had something on them, I could see a close-up and a longer shot of Bob nod and say "Yeah."

"Okay, look at Karen; wave, Karen, I think he forgot which one is you and which is Andy," Jimmie chuckled.

"I can come in there and kick your butt if you want!" I heard Karen's voice come out of a speaker in the console.

"Just kidding. Okay, Bob, you ready?" Jimmie asked.

Bob nodded.

"Okay, Karen, ready to take tape…taking tape, okay, Bob, you're on."

Bob just stared into the camera, immobile, frozen, saying nothing.

"Bob, go ahead, we're taping you," Jimmie said.

Bob just stared into the camera, immobile, frozen, saying nothing.

"Okay, stopping tape. Bob, what's the matter?" Jimmie said.

I watched the screen as Bob blinked, then said, "Nothing, let's go."

Jimmie shrugged, then said, "Okay, Karen, ready to take tape…taking tape, okay, Bob, you're on."

Bob just stared into the camera, immobile, frozen, saying nothing.

"What the hell's he doin'?!" Chuck whispered to me.

"Beats the hell outta me," I told him.

Chuck leaned over Jimmie, pressed a button, and said, "Uhh, Bob? Is there something you don't understand?"

I watched Bob as his voice came through the console.

"No, I'm ready. Let's go before I forget my lines, please." He kept blinking a lot.

Jimmie turned to look at me; all I could do was shrug.

"Go ahead, Jimmie, let's try it again," Chuck said with a sigh.

"Okay, Karen, ready to take tape…taking tape, okay, Bob, you're on."

Nothing.

"Okay, Karen, ready to take tape…taking tape, okay, Bob, you're on."

Nothing; he just stayed there, frozen, staring at the camera. Then we heard the voice of Andy, the other camera operator. "Is this kid weird or what?!"

"Okay, Karen, ready to take tape…taking tape, okay, Bob, you're on."

Nothing.

We tried it a total of fifteen times before I went into the studio and led Bob back into the library. He kept telling me he was ready. I told him we weren't and we'd try it again the next day.

I never did find out what his great commercial was about. The whole thing was more than a little comical; what was to happen the following week was anything but.

9

That previous summer, the same one in which I'd been hired, Page County schools had hired a new football coach and biology teacher to try to get the Mountain Valley High "Fighting Black Bears" football team on the winning side of .500 for the first time in five years. His name was Jack Jorgensen, straight out of the University of Maine, and he was *very* good-looking and *very* single. He'd stayed on at college to get his master's, working as an assistant to his old coach for those two extra years. Somehow, Jack had found his way to northwestern Virginia. Although he was a "Yankee," the local jock-strap contingency had evidently been desperate enough for a winning season that they were willing to look past the outcome of the Civil War...or they didn't know on what side of the Mason-Dixon Line Maine was.

Jack had done what he'd been hired to do; for the first time in recent years, Mountain Valley had had a winning season, had made the districts, won that, and lost by a field goal in the fourth quarter of the regional playoffs.

I liked Jack; he was a good coach, and he was actually a teacher. Most of the other coaches, spread throughout the social-studies department, taught nothing. They'd been hired to coach winning teams, they knew it, and spent most of their classes' time showing movies that had nothing to do with their course content or giving their kids "seatwork" while the coaches worked out game plans, or plays, or whatever full-time high-school coaches and no-time teachers do.

Jack was different; he taught. I know because we had the same planning period that year, and I guessed he'd heard good things about my teaching from kids we shared because sometimes he'd drop by my room during second period and compare notes, or ask for advice about motivating students. At first, I was a little hesitant to give him advice; after all, we were both first-year teachers, but he explained that I was older than he was, and about five years older than most of the rookies, and that he respected me. That meant a lot to me because I respected him for what I'd observed on the sidelines at the home games Sandi and I had attended that fall. He wasn't a screamer or a face-mask grabber; when a player had gotten a penalty, he would take him aside and just talk to him, although I couldn't tell what he said, of course. Or when a kid fumbled or messed up somehow and would come off the field, head down, Jack would do the same thing: take him aside, walk a little with him, arm on the kid's shoulder, then slap the kid on the pads or the ass, and go back to his coaching. I could tell that he wanted to be that kind of teacher in the classroom, too, and I knew he was going to be a real asset to our school.

That all changed because, in our jobs, we still have to deal with adolescents...and their parents.

As I said, he was *very* good-looking and *very* single, and from the moment he'd arrived, the high-school girls had gone silly over his blond good looks and tight, muscular build. Ida Mae had practically wet herself at the first faculty meeting, but I think she realized that she was a little too old for twenty-three-year-old Jack.

He'd met some available local girls at some social functions and at the Presbyterian church he'd begun attending, and had come to one dance that I knew of with one of them, but I guess Jack had been too consumed by amassing a winning record and teaching a bunch of farm boys how to play well and to memorize a playbook with more than four plays in it that dating had taken a seat on the back burner, at least until after football season.

We got wind of the crisis in Jack's life one Tuesday at lunch.

"Hear about Jack Jorgensen?" Ray had asked us.

None of us had.

"What? He's not leavin' is he?!" Wild Bill asked.

"Maybe, but not for a better job," Ray said. "Judi said he's been accused of sexual harassment or something close to that."

"By whom?" Irene asked.

"Some senior girl in his environmental ecology class."

"Who?!" I asked, hoping it wasn't anyone I had.

"Don't know," Ray said. "All Judi heard was that he was accused, by her, of feeling her up or something like that."

"Who the hell would believe that...about *Jack*?!" Deb snapped.

Ray just shrugged. Two days later, the whole school—and probably the whole gossip-riddled county—had heard some version of the story.

What I heard—along with the rest of the people I listened to in that school—was that a girl, whose name was being kept a secret because she was only seventeen, had told her parents that one afternoon, when Jack had had his environmental ecology class down at the school pond, collecting water samples, this girl had told Jack that she felt faint and asked to go lie down on one of the benches set around the edges of the pond, and that Jack had gone to sit with her, and in the process, had reached his hand under her shirt and had fondled her breasts. The girl had told her parents that she had liked it and had even undone her bra for him...and that she thought she was in love with him and that he had told her he loved her.

Needless to say, the manure hit the air-conditioner, the angry parents had called the chairman of the school board and the superintendent, and Jack had been called into Don Dempsey's office, right out of his fourth-period class.

Most of the faculty, except for Ida Mae and a few others, refused to believe it, but that didn't help Jack.

"Jesus, I was on hall patrol an' I saw him when he came outta Don's office!" Bill told us at lunch. "He was pale like a goddam ghost and I never saw anyone look that shook up!"

"Has anyone even heard a hint of who this little bitch is?" Deb asked; since she and Jack rented at the same apartment complex, the two of them had been car-pooling since September and I guess she had gotten closer to him than any of the rest of us. Anyway, she was really steamed.

"I haven't heard anything except for the fifteen versions of the story," Irene said.

"Nope."

"Uh-uh," I said, shaking my head.

"You know damn right well they're gonna screw him, even if they can't prove anything. This is the Bible Belt, you know," Ray added.

"Yeah, Onward Christian Lynchers," Wild Bill said. "Bunch o' goddam hypocrites, an' they're all gonna be comin' outta their caves now, declaring what 'good Christian families they are, blah-blah-blah'!"

The black mood descended on all of us; I could only try to imagine what was going through Jack's mind.

That was all going on, but I had enough weird stuff happening to me to keep my mind off Jack's troubles. First of all, at one point, I was sure *I* was going to get fired and have my one and only year of teaching.

10

See, all year long up to that point, I'd been walking upstairs between my free period (second) and my third-period junior English class and I'd frequently see this couple—a kind of pretty brunette, although with the huge head of hair held tight by a can or two of hair spray, it was easy to tell she came from the local gene pool of NASCAR and Bambi-hunting families—and what was obviously her boyfriend, although he never struck me as much of a "friend" to her. He wore the perpetual greasy-fingerprinted hat, usually advertising "Napa Auto Parts" or "Bass Pro Shops" and he'd be what the kids were calling "in her face" in a corner of the landing on my floor. He had greasy blond hair sticking out from under the cap, and judging by the slope of his forehead and the distance between that and his nose, his family had been in the county for two hundred years, ignoring normal evolution and all intermarrying and swinging from the trees outside their trailers. In other words, he could be the poster boy for *Trailer Trash Redneck*, a magazine that is, fortunately, still unavailable to those of us who can read.

When I'd see him, having backed her into the corner between the railings and the wall, snapping at her in some kind of almost-English, I'd assume he was the typical jealous and insecure teenager, since the two of them made me wonder what a nice girl, despite the hair, wanted to do with someone who seemed to have just fallen out of the evolutionary tree.

One day, I saw her walking down the hall, chattering away with Amy, one of my non-college-bound juniors, and when the moment offered itself, I'd asked her about the girl and the boyfriend.

"Oh, man, Mr. F., that's Sara and Bucky. He's a complete butthole. He accuses her of cheatin' on him every time he sees her even talkin' to another guy. He hits her, too, but she keeps sayin' she loves him. I mean, her family life sucks. Her dad left a year ago an' her mom drinks an' she finds a new bum every month or so to bring home. All Sara wants to do is get married and get outta their trailer, an' she thinks Bucky is the way to do it. I mean, he works at his old man's auto-parts store, so he's got it made as far as the future goes, but he's no good for her."

"Why don't you talk to her? Every time I see them he's yellin' at her with his nose an inch from hers," I asked Amy.

"Oh, man, we've tried to convince her to drop him but all she keeps sayin' is she loves him…*'Oh, I love him so much an' he just has a bad temper!'* Mr. F., you know how many times I've heard that?! She's lost all her best friends but me 'cause they just got sick o' how stupid she is. He's a piece o' sh—well, you know what I mean. Next thing I know, they'll be married—or she'll be pregnant—she'll be having his brats, an' if she's lucky, he might not cheat on her. I just hang around, 'cause without me, she's got no friends."

I just shook my head and thanked Amy for filling me in…and for being such a good friend to someone who was obviously too stupid to know any better.

That wasn't the end of it, though.

Sometime toward the end of that month, I came upstairs, as usual, but this time, he had her against the wall, one hand on her throat and the other hand raised to hit her. She was crying, almost hysterically.

I came up behind him and grabbed the raised hand and told him to let her go. He's not a small guy, maybe an inch taller than my five-ten, and husky. Well, he turned, got this snarly look on his Neanderthal face and took a swing at me, instead.

I'm not a good fighter and never have been; when I was a kid, my way of fighting when I couldn't avoid a fight was to imitate a windmill and then try to tackle the guy, get him on the ground, and then try to kick the hell out of him. But when I was in the Air Force, we had a whole two days of self-defense as part of our "survival" training. Amazingly enough, I found something I was grateful to Uncle Sam's military training for.

In reflex, I'm sure, I blocked his slow, loping swing with my right wrist or forearm (they were both bruised the next morning) and hit him—out of total fear, I'm sure—one shot in the face...or more precisely, in the jaw. Anyway, as I would find out later, it broke his jaw; it also knocked him down. The back of his head hit the tile floor with a very disturbing crack and he was out cold.

I was aware of Sara, the abused girlfriend, screaming and someone grabbing me from behind; I turned to swing again, I think, but it was Ray.

"Jesus Christ, Tom, don't hit *me*! You okay?" he said with an amazed look.

I don't really recall what I did or said; I guess it was the adrenaline or something. I recall breathing really hard and a blur of kids all around us and frozen all along the stairs.

"Don't worry, Mr. Finn, I saw the whole thing," a female voice said. I remember looking around to see Kristi, Jimmie's girlfriend, her bookbag on her back.

"Come on, let's get this guy downstairs," Ray was saying loudly in my right ear. I looked down to see the redneck, now conscious, kneeling on all fours, blood dripping in large dark drops onto the floor.

"Fugg! You bro' muh—ahhh!" he gurgled.

Ray grabbed him under one armpit; I grabbed the other side, and together, we dragged him, feet slipping along each step, to the first floor and the office of one of the assistant principals, Jack Murphy, a crusty administrator about two years from retirement, who had been in World War II and, from what I'd been told, had survived two torpedoed ships and the kamikazes at Okinawa.

I don't remember much after that.

Ray told me the rest, so this is what supposedly happened.
We got good ol' Bucky into Murphy's office, still with blood

running out of his mouth and onto his Big Johnson T-shirt. The conversation went something like:
"What seems to be the problem?" Mr. Murphy had asked, seemingly unperturbed.
"This kid was about to hit his girlfriend. I asked him to stop. He turned and took a swing at me. I guess I hit him," Ray said I said.
"Hmm...I think you did hit him...or he ran into a train, Mr. Finn. Are you okay?" Murphy asked.
Ray says I told him I was, although the next morning, as I already said, I had some bruises and my left hand had three knuckles that were twice their usual size. Sandi had stuck the hand in ice that night but I guess it had been too long since third period. Then Murphy had called the school nurse on the phone, telling her to take her time, that there was no rush. I'm sorry I don't remember that part.
Evidently, Bucky was not unknown to the administrators, and had been suspended a dozen times since ninth grade, which he had repeated twice, as well as his junior year, making Bucky at least nineteen; I guess that's why the school-board disciplinary committee expelled him two weeks later at their monthly meeting. I also got a call from Bucky's mother, telling me that if her husband called, that I should hang up on him and apologizing for her son.
"We can't do nothin' with him at home, neither. He's bigger than his daddy an' he don't know no better'n to be a jackass most o' the time. We're real sorry about this, Mr. Finn. All us Baxters ain't like this!" and then she hung up.
I was still required to appear before the school board to answer any questions they had; Ray and Jack Murphy came with me, as well as Kristi. I told them the whole story, including the history of seeing him yelling at her. They didn't ask me anything or need to ask the three others anything. And that was it.

But it gets better. In the midst to trying to learn to be a teacher, I was still trying to master the art of being a lover.

11

"Tell me something," Sandi said out of the blue one night at another fire, this time with Mr. Hollins Johnson's hickory that was making a fantastic aroma in the night air that we'd just come in from, having sat with her on my lap, the two of us bundled in an old patchwork quilt, as we'd finished the last of a bottle of Australian shiraz. We were on the sofa, Sandi again wearing the Penquins jersey.

"What?"

"How many other ways would you like to make love that we haven't so far?"

"Huh?!"

"Oh, stop stalling. Tell me!" she said.

"Gee, I've been thinking about that question so much lately that you'd think I'd have the answer all ready!" I muttered.

She just sat there, curled up next to me on the small sofa, waiting.

"Okay…in a river—"

"In a river?! How?"

"On a rock…well, like a flat, smooth rock, all smooth from centuries of water running over it."

"And?"

"And what?"

"How?" she asked.

"You really want me to get into this?" I said, somewhat startled by the line of questions. I mean, we had been making love since before Christmas, but hadn't talked a whole lot about it…or during it. We'd experimented, slowly, cautiously, each of us with the other, to see what we liked, what got the right responses. So far, we hadn't found anything we hadn't enjoyed doing to one another...or having done to us. Still...

She waited.

"Okay, okay...I'd lay you on the rock, put your legs over my shoulders, and—"

"Okay, got it. What else?"

"In a meadow full of wildflowers, with bees buzzing all around us...but not stinging us in the ass...on the beach, with the full moon shining...at low tide—"

"Why low tide?" she asked, interrupting.

"So I could hear the sounds coming out of your throat."

"Oh....*Oh*...Go on."

"In the middle of a thunderstorm...no, toward the *end* of one, so we wouldn't get electrocuted in the middle of it all...until you made sounds louder than the thunder."

"Anything else?"

"On a blanket in the middle of a pine forest, with the smell of the needles all around us...on a late spring day...with nobody even nearby to interrupt us."

"Umm...anywhere else?" she asked.

"Yeah, in a barn full of fresh hay—"

"Umm..."

"—in a canoe, on the toilet in the bathroom of a commercial jet, on the desk in my classroom...in a boat, on a goat, over a moat, near a—"

"Now you're just being silly, aren't you?" she asked, tilting her head.

"Yeah."

"You're so goddam romantic it scares me. I would never have thought of that stuff."

"How do you know?" I asked her.

"Think about it. You always start; when I've finished, then I follow your lead, kinda."

"Do I ever tell you what to do?"

"No…it's kinda…kinda like it just comes naturally…you make love to me, then I kinda copy it. That's what I mean, I don't think of anything. I just do what you do."

I thought about it.

"Okay, tell ya what. Next time we're feeling frisky, *you* start."

"Huh?"

"Stop stalling. Next time, *you* decide what we're going to do…where it's all goin'."

She stared at me for half a minute, at least.

"Well, we'll see," is all she said.

About twenty minutes later, she got up to make sure the doors were locked.

"You goin' to bed?" I asked, seeing that it was only approaching nine.

"No." She came in front of me and taking the quilt balled up next to me on the sofa, flipped it open and spread it out in front of the fire. Then she reached behind her neck and pulled the jersey over her head.

The flames flickering in the fireplace set the small tuft of blond hair between her thighs to a golden sheen; then she knelt down on the quilt and beckoned me with a crooked finger. I came to her and let her slide the old shorts down as I stepped out of them.

I watched as she ran her fingers up and down the hair on my chest and belly; then she took it in those same slender fingers and stared at it; then she looked up at me.

"I think it likes me," she whispered.

"I think it's more like it loves you," I gurgled out, seeing a new Sandi begin to emerge. It had always been me who had taken the lead; she had obviously decided that it was time for her to try.

She kissed me there, then touched the tip with her tongue, then she took me, totally and completely. And I began to float. I guess I had to; there was no strength left in my knees by the time I was finished.

When she returned, I lay her on the quilt and took a half-hour to bring her to her climax; each time I felt her rising, I would slow down and kiss her, everywhere, until she started moving her hips and I knew she wanted more. As she lay there, panting quietly, I played with the tiny blond hairs on her belly and made circles in her navel. Then I made love to her again. It might have been that night that I decided I could be happy just doing that to her—and for her—forever.

As I said, I'm still learning…but I'm so goddam romantic, you know?

The next Monday, more news was flying around about Jack's situation.

"They're havin' a closed, super-secret school board meeting this afternoon is what I've heard," Irene said, staring at her cafeteria taco and poking at it with a plastic fork.

"What's the matter with the taco?" I asked her.

"I thought I saw something move," she muttered.

Wild Bill looked up from his cup of yogurt; his wife, he informed us, had decided he'd lost his sexiness because of a growing stomach that was testing the strength of his belt.

"Doesn't she realize that she's the only woman in the world who would ever find you sexy to begin with?" Deb asked with a sly chuckle.

"Hey, Computer Geekette, bite me! I got enough shit with this yogurt without having to put up with needless sarcasm," he growled.

"Oh, wonderful. A guy from Jersey complaining about sarcasm!" Deb replied.

"Hey, lighten up on Jersey!" Irene said through her taco's lettuce.

"Yeah, Joanne's from Jersey, too, remember?" Ray added, referring to his recent bride.

"Okay, okay."

"Anyone heard anything new about Jack's situation?" I asked.

"I heard there was some talk about suspending him with pay but since he's here today, I guess they decided not to do that," Bill told us.

"Sure, why pay him when they're not getting their money's worth, right?" Irene said.

"Hey, c'mon guys, the school board's usually pretty supportive of us. It's the board of supervisors who're a bunch of assholes. All they care about is property taxes," Ray asserted.

"Of course, since most of them own thousands of acres," I said.

"Yeah, and all inherited. Those shitheads couldn't afford ten acres if they had to buy them with the dickhead jobs they all work. There isn't a self-made wealthy person in this whole county…every one inherited whatever they got," Bill said.

I guess all of us—outsiders to the whole local culture—agreed, because that part of the conversation died.

"Anyway, I hear Jack's hadda hire a lawyer from Harrisonburg," Ray said.

"Yeah, I guess local ones wouldn't wanna touch this 'cause it might hurt business," Deb suggested. "He won't talk to me about the whole thing…says it would just upset me…an' get him more pissed off. At least, that's what he says."

"I just can't believe that no one knows who this girl is that accused him. Since when can anyone keep anything a secret around here?" I asked.

"Oh, I think it's gonna come out eventually, but maybe not before the trial," Irene said.

"*Trial*?! What trial?" a couple of us said at the same time.

"Well, I heard that the parents are planning to sue Jack for something like causing emotional damage to their daughter or somethin' like that."

"How can he even afford a lawyer on a first-year teacher's salary?!" Irene asked. "Shit, we make less than a starting post-office worker!"

"Well, you might also consider the fact that he might not be a first-year teacher much longer if the school board decides to believe the mystery slut," Ray offered.

"You know, this whole thing is getting me more and more pissed off!" I said, standing up and tossing my lunch bag into the garbage.

I left, hoping I wasn't going to carry my suddenly shitty mood into fifth-period creative writing.

12

Fortunately, even if it was momentary, a little comic relief made its way into my life an hour later, during my sixth-period class, the "non-academic" class of juniors, most of whom were just not planning to attend college.

Even as a rookie teacher, I'd found out very quickly that labels for kids—and whole classes—didn't necessarily fit, or belong. Although this bunch was considered non-college-bound and therefore, "non-academic," they could be as "academic" as they were challenged to be. After two or three weeks at the beginning of the school year, I had quickly determined that I would not have to prepare lesson plans for the sixth-period class that were different from the ones for my two "accelerated" junior classes. The sixth-period kids were perfectly capable of handling the same work, could understand the same literature, and didn't need any more grammar and punctuation instruction than the advanced students, who were just as ignorant about when to use *good* vs. *well*, or *fewer* vs. *less* as the others.

My biggest challenge was in getting the non-academics to read anything that had to be done outside of class. I've never been a proponent of having a class full of teenagers sitting like lumps, books open, while either the teacher or other students read aloud. For the most part, the kids may have their books open, but they're not reading along; most aren't even paying attention. The only things open are the books; their minds aren't.

So, in order to get the kids to do reading outside of class, I had them take chapter-by-chapter notes, and let them use them on a twenty-question true-false quiz the day the book was due. It was a simple test, and just by eyeballing their answers, I could tell if a kid hadn't read it. For example, on the quiz on *Adventures of Huckleberry Finn*, I'd made up absurd statements, such as "When Jim found Huck in the cave with Maisie Lou, Jim was jealous," and "In the end, Pap forgave Huck for killing his dog." Any kid who'd answer "true" to those would be courteously told to take the novel and his notebook, go outside the class, and come back in to take another quiz when he'd actually finished the book. I only had to do that once or twice for the whole class to witness for the students to decide that it was much better to read the books I gave them than to be embarrassed in front of their peers; it also gave the kids who *had* read the book a sense of fairness, since most of them resented kids who'd never read the material but could listen in well enough during discussions to still pass tests on the book after all the discussions had ended.

Still, in any "non-academic" class, there were some students who deserved the title "non-academic," mostly because they were lazy, or ignorant and content to stay that way. Such was the case with a girl I'd tried to tolerate all year, a girl we'll call Tammy.

Tammy was one of those Southern girls with the hair-sprayed bottle-blond explosion, complete with about an inch of dark roots showing. Tammy had spent most of the year so far flipping through fashion catalogs and ones for cosmetics instead of doing anything academic, and had firmly maintained an average of 70, just enough to avoid summer school. On more than one occasion, Tammy had let us all know that her future career goal was marriage, although her most recent boyfriend had been kicked out of school and had subsequently joined the Navy after getting his GED.

Anyway, on this particular day, most of the kids, who'd had Mr. Ketchum for American history, had come into class still debating—or arguing—an issue that Ketchum (one of the few social-studies teachers who actually taught) had brought up the period before: what to do about terrorists.

Well, Dylan and Todd were arguing that we should send Navy SEAL units into Afghanistan, which our government had determined was harboring terrorists and actually hosted terrorist-training camps.

Other kids thought we should resort to other measures.

"You're crazy! Just send in a bunch o' missiles and B-52's an' bomb the crapola outta the whole country!" Calvin insisted.

"But you'd kill kids and women and poor people who just live there! You can't just bomb a whole country!" a different Tammy argued.

"Why not? What's Afghanistan good for?" Calvin replied.

"I think we should get the United Nations to do something," a girl named Katherine suggested.

"Yeah, right! They got about as much clout as a fruit-fly's fart!" Dylan told her.

"Hey, what do *you* think we should do about it, Mr. Finn?" Todd asked. I just shrugged.

"Beats me. If the geniuses in Washington can't decide what's best, I'm sure not gonna make any suggestions," I told him.

It was at that point that Tammy, whose limited cerebral concentration must have been disrupted by all the shouting and debate, looked up from her Mary Kay catalog with an annoyed look and said, to no one in particular,

"What are y'all making such a fuss over?!"

"Afghanistan, Tammy, you know, the country that's been in the news for like a year now," Todd explained.

"Aff-who?" she asked, blinking her two-inch-long fake eyelashes moronically.

"Jees-*us*, Tammy, Afghanistan. Here, see?!" Dylan said, going over to the map of the world that I had on one wall and putting his finger on the country.

"Where's that?" she asked.

"Right here, you moron! Where my finger is! In Asia!! Jees-us, don't you ever watch the news or read *Newsweek* or anything?!" Dylan yelled, getting more agitated than ever.

By this time, every kid in the class was staring at her in disbelief. I mean, the topic of that country and others in the Middle East had dominated the news since forever.

"How could you possibly not have heard of Afghanistan?!" Katherine asked her.

In a huff, Tammy summoned up every ounce of her formidable logic, and snapped,

"Well, I'm sure there are people in Aff-wherever who never heard of *Luray*, either!!"

In the stunned silence that followed that brilliant statement, you could've heard a bowling ball drop. Dylan looked at Todd, they stared back at Tammy, who'd turned back to her catalog, everyone turned to look at me for some kind of typical Finn snappy comment. All I could do was shake my head and shrug.

"Okay, well, how about getting out last night's homework on hyphens and we'll see if you guys understand when to use them."

And so it went. At least, it helped me to forget Jack Jorgensen's problems for the rest of the day.

As I was about to get into Baby in the teacher's lot that day, I saw a slip of paper out of the corner of my eye, stuck under the driver's side windshield wiper.

Opening it up, I read, *Hey, Sexy, I want you and I want to do things with you. xxxooo.*

At first, it looked a little like Sandi's handwriting, but then I realized that the note-writer put little bubbles over the *i*'s, plus a split second later I reminded myself that Sandi was at JMU right then and not working in the cafeteria at MVHS anymore.

"Oh, great, a crush," I muttered, folding up the small piece of paper and putting it in my shirt pocket. "Just what I need."

I showed her the note when she got home from school; she thought it was "cute."

"Hey, dummy, considering what's happened to Jack Jorgensen recently, the last thing I want or need is some teeny-bopper thinking she wants to do 'things' with me!" I growled.

Sandi just giggled a little.

"Well, *I* want to do things with you, so why wouldn't some other female with the same good taste?" she asked with a mischievous look, refusing to take the whole thing any more seriously.

"Whatever!" I snapped, rolling the note up into a little ball and tossing it into the fireplace.

For the rest of that week, I tried to play detective and figure out who the note-writer was, especially since every day after that, except for Wednesday, when it had poured all day, I found a new note, usually telling me I was "hot" or that the two of us could "make hot music together." I kept looking for furtive glances coming at me from some girl, or a shy smile maybe, but nothing happened to give me any reason to believe it was one of my girls.

"Maybe she's not in your classes," Sandi suggested one night.

"Yeah, I thought of that; I don't know," I mumbled between bites of the pizza that she'd picked up at Anthony's, out on Route 211, on the way home that Friday night.

"Or maybe it's a female teacher."

"Naah, the bubbles over her *i*'s is a tip-off. That's a sure sign of an adolescent. Grown women get out of that habit," I told her with conviction.

"Well, she's gonna reveal herself sooner or later," Sandi concluded.

After a moment or two of reflection, I said, "Y'know, with the Jack shit going on, maybe to protect myself, I oughta show Don the notes so someone knows ahead of time that I'm not interested."

"I doubt that he'd do anything. He probably would just laugh it off as a teenage crush, wouldn't he?" she asked.

"Well, yeah, probably, but that's what I'd want him to do…and know that that's what I considered it."

So I made up my mind that I'd tell Don, my principal, about it after school on Monday, once I'd checked to see if she'd left a note for me to show him; otherwise, I'd just fill him in on the history so far.

So much for plans: as I was getting ready to leave my classroom that Monday afternoon, *she* walked in to identify herself instead.

13

Looking up, I saw her standing there.

"Something I can do for you, M.D.?" I asked.

Closing the door behind her, she formed what I'd call a smirk with her full lips and said, "Well, you could tear off all my clothes and lick me all over, but maybe we should do that somewhere more intimate. Whaddaya think?"

My mouth went completely dry, I felt my heart crawl up to replace my Adam's apple, and I think I recall a weakening in my knees. I do recall that I sat back down in my chair.

She came slowly toward me, running her tongue along her lips. She was wearing an especially low top that exposed about three inches of cleavage; the pants were another pair she'd sprayed on. She hadn't been wearing that top in class earlier that day.

As she got to the front of my desk, I got up—amazingly quickly—and went to open the door again, stepping out into the hall as well. She followed.

"Oh, come on, Tom, are you telling me I'm not hot and that you'd turn down the chance to be with me?" she asked in a very fake, husky voice. I wondered which soap operas she watched.

"M.D., I'm very flattered. I'm also very engaged and very much in love with my fiancée, so—"

"I'm not lookin' for ya to fall in love with me or leave your precious fiancée, I just wanna have a kinda affair with you, that's all."

In the midst of this momentary crisis, I still wanted to ask her what a "kinda affair" was like. Before I could say anything, she continued.

"Look, before my fathah moved us to this shithole, I hung around with a lot older crowd in New Yawk an' I'm a lot more mature than these manure tossers around heah, an' I'm a woman wit' needs, know what I mean?"

It was obvious that she'd rehearsed what argument she was going to use because she just kept going, all in a very low tone while we stood there in the empty hallway.

"Look," she continued, "I'm not gonna say anything, I'm not gonna be like that psycho in *Fatal Attraction* or whatever that movie was, I'm not gonna call ya up and bug ya, I just wanna get it on a few times—you know, do you, let you do me, have some friggin' fun, know what I mean?!"

I really wanted to laugh; she was *not* mature, she was certainly not a *woman*—despite the woman's ripe body—and I didn't trust her one bit.

"Look, M.D., forget it, okay? I'm really flattered, really I am. If I was sixteen or seventeen again, I—"

"I don't want some friggin' sixteen- or seventeen-year-old dipshit, I want *you* an' your twenty-something body. Jesus Christ, pal, what the hell's your problem? I'm not demandin' anything except some satisfyin' sex for both of us!" she snapped, getting somewhat louder at the same time. She quickly stopped when we both heard someone coming.

Just then, Mr. Jeck, pushing a wide broom, turned the corner of the hallway and came toward us. As he got nearer, he looked up at me and stopping, squinted at me and asked, "Hey, Conners, you know how to make angel-food cake?"

"I'm not Mr. Conners," I told him, aware of some melodramatic deep sighs coming from M.D. "And no, I don't know how to make angel-food cake," I added.

"Angel-food cake? Who cares about *angel-food cake*?!" Jeck snapped, scratching the gray stubble on his chin and moving on with his push-broom.

"*I wonder if he's related to Mabel Dunbar,*" I thought.

Leaving the two of us still standing outside my door, I could see that debating the issue was not going to get me anywhere; I was totally reluctant to going back into my classroom again because I knew she'd follow and try to close the door...and maybe try more than that to prove her point, so I just shook my head and brushed by her and headed for the stairs. Amazingly enough, she didn't attempt to follow.

I headed straight for Don Dempsey's office, only to be told by his secretary that he'd left at one o'clock to attend some function at the school-board office.

"Shit!" I said to myself. I left him a note, hoping that he'd return to the high school before going home.

Then I hopped in Baby, finding no note, and left.

"So, should I worry...or are you really gonna turn down red-hot sex with someone you make sound like a young Sophia Loren?" Sandi asked right after she'd gotten home and I'd filled her in.

"Damn it, this isn't some kind of a joke!" I snapped. "This could turn out really bad. Suppose she pulls the same shit as that other girl with Jack an' tells her mob-connected old man that we've done something, or that *I* was the one who came on to *her*?!! Have you thought of that?!"

That she hadn't was obvious when the twinkle in the blue eyes and the smile went away in a snap.

"Okay, okay...shit, it *could* turn out bad, couldn't it?" Sandi said slowly.

I picked up the phone in the bedroom.

"Who you callin'?"

"Don. I left him a note but he must've gone straight home."

All I got was an answering machine; I left a message, asking him to call me. I thought about trying to let him know what it was about, but I didn't know exactly how to put it in a brief message. I hung up and hoped he'd call. Stuff was zooming through my mind faster than I could keep up with it.

"*...Everyone in the damn county seemed to know about the Knopfs, so they'd all be ready to believe another teacher was messin'* *around with one of his students...an' the shit with Jack is still up in the air...what the hell am I gonna do?...where the hell's Don?!"*

I became aware of her kneeling behind me on the bed, massaging my shoulders and trying to get the tension out of them.

"I'm all right," I told her.

"Yeah, an' I'm Oprah!" she said sarcastically. "Your shoulders and neck feel like steel! Relax already!"

"I can't, dammit! All I can see is my whole goddam career going down in flames because of some horny Italian witch who has convinced herself she's an adult an' wants to have a 'kinda affair' with me!"

"Look, when the principal calls, you can just tell him what happened," she tried to assure me.

"Yeah, fine, but where the hell *is* he? For all I know, M.D.'s home telling her bullshit and the phone's gonna start ringing in all the wrong places!"

The phone never rang that night. And I didn't get much sleep.

The next morning, I got to school extra early, even for me. The clock read 6:51 when I opened the door to the main office and sat down. My guts felt like they were doing laundry; my eyes felt as if someone had pissed in them and my mouth was very, very dry. I must've gone out in the hall half a dozen times to the water fountain by the time Don came in at 7:20.

His eyebrows went up a little when he saw me waiting.

"Well, hi, Tom, what's up? Problem? Not another kidnapped student, I hope!" he asked as he stuck his bagged lunch in the small refrigerator in the corner of the office.

"No, but yeah, a problem, an' I need to let you know about it before it gets any bigger."

The eyebrows went up a little higher.

"Hmm...okay, come on in," he said, stepping aside and holding his door open for me.

I told him.

"Hmm…it's good that you're filling me in now…and you're right, this could become a problem. Look, I have to ask: you've done nothing to encourage this girl, right? No 'come talk to me after school' or stuff like that, no matter how innocent on your part?"

He could see that his question angered me.

Holding up a hand, he continued.

"Look, it's the same kind of question you're gonna be asked if anything comes of this. I said I had to ask. I don't think you're that stupid, plus I know you're engaged, so just talk and try to relax, okay?"

Easy for him to say. Anyway, I assured him that I'd hardly said fifty words to M.D. since she'd arrived.

"She spends most of every class lookin' out the window and lookin' pissed off, Don. I mean, she does her work, but never gets involved in class discussions. She's made it really clear that she hates it here, she hates her parents for bringing her here, and she's made no attempt, at all, to make any friends. That's why this whole thing blew me away! She hardly ever even looks at me!" I said, feeling more and more helpless.

"Okay. Maybe I ought to give the parents a call. Whaddaya think?"

"I don't know. If she hasn't said anything, I'd hate to get the whole thing started."

"Yeah, but if we tell them about the notes and—"

"But I didn't save any of them, so it'll just be my word against hers, an' I have a feeling that they might wanna believe her rather than believe she's a conniving liar and all," I explained.

He took a deep breath, leaning back in his high-backed leather chair.

"Okay, okay…let's leave it at this: type up a list of the notes and what you recall them saying, the conversation yesterday, an' I'll keep it on file in case anything comes up."

Well, it wasn't what I'd hoped for, but then again, I'd had no idea what to do.

I was trying to put it all out of my mind when I got to my room and found a longer note from her, sitting in the middle of my desk.

14

Dear Tom,
    I'm sorry if you think you don't love me, I think I love you. I really do,
    I know you think I'm some spoiled slutty bitch but, the only thing that makes me glad I'm here is you. When I look at you my heart leaps out of my chest. I want you to touch me, kiss me, lay on me. I want you to make love to me untill I scream. I know you want the same, why do you deny what you know you want.
    I don't expect anything from you. Just physical things. You know I have a great body so why would you turn down such a simple offer. I know your not gay cause your engaged. Please just be with me, maybe only a couple times. I know someplace we can be alone. Then I will leave you alone. I promise. I don't expect any more then that.

You know who. xxxooo

With another totally dry mouth, I took the note down to Don.

"I wish she'd handwritten it instead of printing it out from a computer," he said.

"What difference does it make?" I asked, fighting the feeling of loose bowels.

"Well, it just would make it easier," he said slowly.

"Easier than *what*?!"

"Oh, I don't know. Handwriting, you know...okay, look, Tom, just try to relax. I'll hang onto this. I still want you to write up the other stuff ASAP, okay?" he said, sliding the note to one corner of his large, glass-topped desk.

"Yeah, I'll get on it during my planning period an' get it to you then."

I left, but I carried that sinking feeling of doom with me.

I got the facts to Don during my planning period but dreaded walking into third period.

Almost everyone had arrived when M.D. walked in. The change in her was incredible; everyone noticed and a buzzing started up throughout the room.

The tight clothes, the jewelry, the glamour hairdo—they were all gone. She wore a plain pair of jeans, a loose T-shirt with a dolphin on it, and a pair of Nikes or some other athletic brand. The hair, parted to one side, was brushed back behind her bare ears and held in place with small blue plastic clips. And hardly any makeup. Maybe something around her eyes, some lipstick—but nothing like the overkill of before. There was nothing she could do about the body, but she had obviously done nothing to call attention to it, either.

She smiled slightly at me as she went to take her seat in the back, working very hard at not noticing that every kid in the class was gawking at her transformation. I had a hell of a time keeping them— and me—on task for that class. Fortunately, half the period was devoted to a brief videotape I'd made from a Bob Vila *This Old House* episode about Plymouth Plantation; I purposely avoided looking M.D.'s way for the remainder of the period.

My momentary feeling of relief and rescue lasted no longer than the end of the class. She sat back there until everyone had left but her. Then she got up to leave, pausing at my desk.

"Do you like me better this way? Do I look less slutty? More homey-like?" she asked very softly.

"M.D., I like you. You look fine. Let's just keep it this way, okay?

I'm your teacher, you're my student...nothing else," I tried.
"Did you get my note?"
"Yes."
"Well?"
"No. Look, M.D., I—" I was going to tell her that I'd brought the matter to Don's attention, but she just stormed out, slamming the door behind her.
"*Shit*!" I thought.
Don stopped by after the final bell rang.
"Tom, got a call from Mr. Battaglia. He wants a parent conference tomorrow...during your planning period. Hey, it's okay, you're covered, remember?" he said, trying to reassure me but he did nothing to remove the horrible, gut-churning feeling.
"What did you tell him? What did he say?"
"He just said he got a call on his cell phone and that his daughter was very upset about something that had to do with you. I told him I was aware of a certain matter but I didn't give him any more than that. The less he knows, the less he can talk to the daughter about and the less she can fabricate ahead of time. Let's just wait until tomorrow morning, okay?"
"Yeah, right!"
"Just try to relax...this is nothing new."
"It is for *me*," I told Don. "And on top of what Jack's goin' through!"
Don came over and put a hand on my shoulder.
"Hey, I don't need this crap, either. It's okay. We'll take care of it, all right? Try to get some sleep and have all your facts ready tomorrow."
"Is *she* gonna be at the conference, too?"
"Yes, both parents, the daughter, you and me."
"Oh, great!"
"Relax, it'll be all right!" Don repeated. I didn't believe him; I don't think he was all that sure about it, either.

Thanks to Sandi's massage, an order of mussels marinara and another great pizza from Anthony's—oh, yeah, plus two martinis and a couple beers to try to numb my mind—I did actually get about two hours sleep that night…before I woke up and the thoughts and worries started up all over again.

The next day was going to be a significant one in my young life; things were going to shift a little in the Jack Jorgensen situation, too, but that would have to wait until the following Sunday.

Gerry Battaglia was nothing as I had expected him to be. Don't get me wrong, I grew up around a lot of Italian kids, so my knowledge of that particular ethnic group is not restricted to the *Godfather* trilogy and other films about the mob and the Mafia. I guess it was just that his being in construction, although Wild Bill had told us that he didn't actually do construction, had formed an image in my mind of a guy with a bull neck, lots of gold, and wide shoulders. He was none of those.

When I walked into Don's office at the beginning of second period, I saw M.D., dressed very conservatively, a thin, dark-haired woman in her early forties or late thirties, a purse on her lap, and a tall, trim man the same approximate age. He looked more like a tennis pro or a golf instructor.

Don introduced us; Gerry Battaglia was about two or three inches taller than my five-ten, wore a three-button maroon knit shirt and a pair of pleated—and very expensive, I'm sure—tan slacks. He had the same hair as Mark: dark brown, wavy, a little gray here and there—the kind the barber would just run a sharp razor through and it would be done. His handshake was firm and dry, but the smile was disarming.

Despite my reservations, I believed the smile was genuine, if somewhat hesitant, almost embarrassed. But the eyes were something else; like Mark's as well, they were penetrating, dark, and intense. The anger I'd expected to see was absent.

"Mr. Finn. Sorry about this, but…" That's all he said; Mrs. Battaglia looked the embarrassed that Deb had described from her own conference over the referral M.D. had received. Battaglia sat back down; Don gestured me to do the same.

Don asked the Battaglias to begin the conversation.

Mr. Battaglia cleared his throat, looked quickly at his daughter, and then said, "Well, Maureen called me yesterday with a very interesting story. According to her, Mr. Finn here has made several advances toward her, implying that he'd like to get more than a little friendly with Maureen...way beyond the normal relationship between teacher and student. So, obviously, that's why we're here."

"Why don't we let Maureen tell us about that," Don asked quietly.

She looked somewhat shocked; I think she figured that all it was going to take was her parents to come, raising hell, and that would fix me.

"Me?!" she kind of croaked.

"Yeah, go ahead, tell them what you told me," Gerry Battaglia told her.

The silence must have lasted at least thirty seconds before she spoke.

"Uhh, well, Mr. Finn kinda asked me to come in after school to talk about my essays an'...uhh, well, I did an' he...uhh...told me he found me real attractive an' wondered why I didn't have a boyfriend...uhh...and another time, after class, he asked me to stay after the other students left an' he kinda tol' me he thought I was sexy an' asked if I needed a ride home, you know?"

I was about to open my mouth when I caught Don out of the corner of my eye shaking his head briefly.

"Mr. Finn?" Gerry Battaglia asked, those dark eyes right on mine.

"I don't know what to say. If you came here, fully believing your daughter, then there's not a lot I can say or do. I brought this situation up to Mr. Dempsey earlier when I found notes on my car and eventually found out that M.D. had left them."

"Notes that said what?" Battaglia asked, taking another quick glance at his daughter.

"Telling me I'm sexy, or that she wanted to do 'things' with me, stuff like that."

"How are you so sure it was my daughter?"

"She came into my room after school last week and told me."

Well, the mother sucked in her breath so hard that I thought papers were going to fly off Don's desk.

"I don't believe it!" she gasped.

The Drano feeling in my guts began to get worse, and I recall wondering if it was possible to get an instant ulcer.

"She also left me a note the same day; it was there when I got to school the following morning," I informed them as I watched Don produce it and hand it to the father.

"I didn't write that! I didn't write anything!" M.D. insisted, but her voice was shaky and her eyes were darting back and forth between her father and me. The mother was looking at M.D. very intently.

He read the note, looked at his daughter, seemed to read it again, handed it to his wife, and then looked over at me.

"Hard to tell who wrote it, since it's not handwritten; you could have written this yourself, couldn't you?" he asked me, again with that penetrating gaze.

"Well, I could have, but I doubt I would have made that many mistakes," I told him.

"You could've made them just for that reason, so it would look like an English teacher couldn't have written it," he challenged, but still, without any anger or antagonistic expression.

"Tell you what: why don't you read that note to M.D. and have her write it down; if the same mistakes appear—and I'm sure *she* didn't make any of them intentionally—that might convince you," I suggested, wondering how I'd been able to think that clearly when it felt as though a thousand hornets were buzzing around inside my mind.

So Don pulled out a pad from a desk drawer, stood up and took it to M.D., along with a pen. Then Mr. Battaglia began to read the note to his daughter. Her hand was shaking, too.

15

It didn't take long for the truth to come out. As I had hoped, M.D. made the same mistakes, using the wrong *your* instead of *you're*, *lay* instead of *lie*, the same wrong or missing punctuation, and the other errors. I think the "spoiled slutty bitch" did it for the parents, though; Mr. Battaglia had turned to her at the point of reading that to her and had said, "Maureen, I seem to recall that you used the same exact phrase during that argument the three of us had the other night."

Finally, M.D. just broke down in tears, wailing about being sorry, saying she didn't know what's wrong with her, and still trying to insist that she thought she was in love with me.

It was at that point that Battaglia had turned to Don and had said, "If it's all right with you, we'll go now." Then, turning to me, he just shrugged and said, "I'm sorry."

"Me, too," I told him. Then they left, the mother pushing M.D. out ahead of her, the father closing the door behind them.

"Whew!" Don said, dropping down into his chair.

"Yeah," I muttered.

"You okay?" he asked. "You have a class next period, don't you?"

"Yeah, the one *she's* in."

"I don't think she's gonna show up today. I have a feeling they have some issues with their daughter that they're gonna be addressing for the rest of the day...and maybe after that."

"Yeah, most likely. Hey, Don, you know, something just occurred to me, now that I don't have images of being fired—or worse—flashing through my mind. Do you think she's the one who accused Jack?"

He shook his head.

"No, I was informed who the girl in that situation is, although I can't discuss any more than that. *Those* parents wouldn't even come in and talk to me...or Jack. They went straight to the school board and the super...and then to a lawyer. I wish Jack's problem could get solved as easily as yours," he said with a long sigh.

Needless to say, I made my way to my room with a distinct sense of having a thousand-pound boulder lifted from my back.

M.D. wasn't in class that period, and didn't return to school for the rest of the week. I wanted to ask Mark about it, but didn't know how to bring the subject up delicately. I was kind of hoping he'd say something, but he didn't. He did come to class on the day following the conference and gave me a little shrug and what I read as an apologetic raise of his eyebrows. It seemed as though a lot of people were doing a lot of shrugging lately.

By the time I'd gotten home, I was emotionally exhausted. The sleeplessness, the anxiety, the worry—all of the scenarios I'd imagined, in which nothing turned out right—had simply worn me out. I think Sandi knew it, too.

I was asleep on the sofa when she got in; she woke me up, and taking me by the wrist, led me into the bedroom, stripped me down despite my protests that I was fine, and sent me into the shower, following a minute later with two bottles of Corona Lights—not the best thing to take into a shower, I know, but...

In the bed a while later, she massaged my back, slowly, deliberately, first pressing her fists' knuckles hard into my muscles, then spreading her fingers and stroking my back as though she were playing a harp, maybe. Then she had me roll over and slowly, deliberately, made love to me, all the time whispering to me.

"I love you...this is what love is like...do you feel my love coming through my fingers...through my lips?...Shhh, don't say a word...do you feel lighter? Smile if you do (I did and I did)...My Tom...Tom...no one here but us...feel like air...we are lighter than air..."

I fell asleep listening to her, feeling her lips on me, her fingers running lightly through the field of hair on my chest...that's how I fell asleep.

It was the first night in a while that I slept straight through...or slept that many hours.

I awoke the next morning when the sun was just turning the curtains a thin gray; a few early robins were making a fuss over something. I turned my head to see her, chin on her palm, leaning on an elbow, looking down at me.

"I love you, you know," she whispered some more.

"I know; that's all I'll ever need," I replied.

She laughed a little, kissed me on the forehead and the tip of my nose, and got out of bed.

"You need more than me...but you have at least that much so far," she said, going out to make the coffee.

I looked at my watch. It was just six o'clock; it was also the first of April, and spring was definitely in the air that morning when I opened the back door and took a deep breath.

Spring in Virginia, my favorite season. Down here, it lasts a long while. First, we have crocuses and daffodils peeking through, sometimes with some snow still on the ground in the shady spots. Then we have to wait for one stretch of about two days of warm weather, like in the mid-fifties or above, then a good dose of rain: and then the world explodes! We'll have a thunderstorm one afternoon and after it, I'll hear "peepers" (tiny, baby frogs...don't remember hearing them in semi-urban Pennsylvania...maybe on my grandparents' farm) echoing from the woods and creek behind the cabin, at the base of Mom, our mountain. After that rain-warmth cycle, the first color will be the swelling leaf-buds on the trees—maple, oak, beech, sweet gum, birch, sycamore, linden, pin oak, hickory—to add to the green that hangs around all year in the hemlocks, pines, cedars, and spruces. Then the leaves appear, first light green, then darker; then the first color.

There are these slender trees down here called Eastern redbuds...the flowers hang in grape-like clusters and are really more purple than red; about the time they're fading, the dogwoods—the state tree—explode into white flowers and grow wild all over the landscape, as do the native redbuds. By the time the dogwoods are fading, all the flowering shrubs—lilacs, azaleas, rhododendrons, camellias—pop open. Then all we—Becky, Pop, Sandi, Ronnie and I— have to do is go to a nursery and come home and plant the annuals—marigolds, zinnias, impatiens—and by that time, it's time for me to take my turn at tilling the 6,000-square-foot garden and get in my beloved tomatoes, eggplants, peppers—twenty kinds of hot ones—and the stuff I'll grow for others: squash (which I'll grow for everyone else but personally refuse to eat; as Russell Baker once wrote, "Squash is the only vegetable that tastes like it sounds"), beets, beans and sugar peas (I'll eat *them*), and ten or fifteen different herbs—rosemary and oregano grow all year. Pop and I argue sometimes about who plants what and how much to plant, but it's a fun kind of arguing; after all, it feeds all of us, plus Ray and Joanne chip in with the work and take from the garden as well.

What I love most, maybe, are the aromas of spring; sometimes, the air smells scented from all the flora, but often, it just carries a crispness that makes me want to suck in cubic yards of it. And the nights! It gets windy a lot through early May, and the stars, unaffected by the ground lights (there aren't any) are spectacular, like the night skies I remember as a boy...or on dark, moonless, windy nights in summer and winter in Pennsylvania, even in the last years I lived there, at home and at college. Some nights, the Milky Way looks as if God took a finger and smeared cream across the darkness. Before the leaves mature, on a full-moon night, the shadows of the trees stretch out forever, and we can walk our quiet country property and the paths up the mountain as if it were broad daylight...or narrow daylight.

On our tiny back porch, we can sit out there at night and listen to the night sounds of owls and whippoorwills off in the trees, and the coons and possums and skunks snuffling around in the leaves. That lasts until summer arrives and the 'skeeters move in...and we have to move back inside. Even the cabin smells clean, like laundry dried on the line outside, when we can open the windows and let the world blow through. I guess I come back alive with the spring; I'm so dormant, like the plant world, in the winter. The only exercise I can get is splitting some of the wood that's still too big and carrying it in...and my one- or two-mile walk every other day when Sandi's in the mood. The first semi-warm day will find me outside, doing *anything,* just to be outdoors. If I were still in Pennsylvania, that'd be the day I'd be out spreading fertilizer on Pop's old postage-stamp-sized lawn or cleaning out the garage.

As I've said, Virginia's a good place to be...all year long, but especially in the spring.

Even on April Fool's Day.

16

When I got to school that morning, I found a memo in my mailbox; well, the same memo was in everyone's mailbox.

It was from Hartley, the new assistant principal who had arrived when I did, who had been given all the grunt jobs, including making up the duty roster for teachers. Hartley and I rarely crossed paths; his office was in the vocational wing and his other duties had nothing to do with me. It was pretty widely agreed upon that Hartley was at MVHS for no more than a year or two of résumé-building before he would set his sights on a principalship at some other school.

> TO: Faculty
> FROM: Mr. A.H.T. Hartley (The first two initials had gotten considerable discussion among the Lunch Bunch—and others, I'm sure—as to what they stood for)
> RE: Teacher Duty Assignments
>
> It has come to my attention that some faculty members are NOT going to their duty assignments when assigned. It is essential that ALL teachers do their assigned duty assignments. We cannot maintain consistency among faculty members if ALL faculty are NOT doing their duty.
>
> Please report to your assigned duties immediately.

"You know, I couldn't go to my assigned duty 'immediately' because I read that memo at 7:45 this morning an' my duty isn't until between fifth and sixth period," Irene said sarcastically.

"Me neither," Deb told her, "mine's *after* school—duh!"

"Tom, you think old A.H. has a problem with redundancy?" Ray asked me.

"No."

"*No*!!??"

"No. I don't even think he knows what the word means," I replied.

After the brief laughter died, Wild Bill said, "Well, I know I wanna do *my* duty because it's an *assigned* duty and it's my duty to do the duty that has been *assigned* to me as my *assignment*, so I'm gonna—*ouch*!"

"Shuddup! You even *sound* like Hartley!" Irene told him, removing her long nails from his left forearm.

"Y'know, I get pissed off when we get one of these generalized blanket statements that don't apply to all of us. I know Tom and I go to our smoke-check duty, an' so do you guys," Ray said.

I thought about it for a minute.

"Hey, Ray, we both have duty between second and third, right?" I said.

"Yeah. I got the back-hall boys' room."

"Well, I've got the boys' room at the end of my floor, but I managed to flush all the smokers outta there, but some o' my guys complain that they're now down in the first-floor bathroom by guidance, an' that's the one that Spengler has and I know he never checks out that john 'cause he's one of those who don't go to their *assigned* duties."

"So?"

"I also know that when the smokers hear the door open, they wait for the password."

"What password?" Ray asked.

"Smokers say 'it's cool' an' the smokers go right back to

smoking," I explained.

"Hmm, having some trouble with redundancy there, Tom," Irene snickered.

"Shuddup! Anyway, how about you come down an' meet me there at the end of second today an' we'll snag a bunch o' them? Then we can march them down to Hartley and *present* him with a *present*," I suggested, looking directly into Irene's blue eyes.

"Okay. Let's do it."

So I met Ray inside the doors at the bottom of the first-floor stairs so none of the not-so-clever smokers making their way through the door to the lavatory would see two male teachers standing outside the john. We gave them about two minutes to light up and get comfortable as a few late arrivals entered. Then I went in, leaving Ray, who's a good six-two and about an even two hundred solid cross-country-skiing pounds outside the door in case anyone inside decided to bolt. And in I went.

"It's cool," I said in a different voice.

I was a little surprised at what I saw. See, as you enter the bathroom, there's a narrow, short hall, I guess you'd call it, with the sinks all along the right wall. Where the room opened up to the left, the urinals were on both walls closest to the door, three on that wall and three more on half of the left wall. The rest of the left wall was taken up by two toilet stalls without doors.

Well, crammed into the two open stalls were sixteen guys, about nine or ten in the one closest to the open window, the rest in the stall closest to me as I entered. The cloud of cigarette smoke looked as if a small smokestack from a factory was somewhere in the small room; the heaviness of the humid air of the school just let it hang there, despite the fact that the guys in the furthest stall had the tilt-window open as far as it would go.

Our smoking jackasses had relaxed once they'd heard my "it's cool" so they kind of jumped when I said, "All right, guys, put 'em out an' let's take a little walk to the assistant principal's office."

"Shit!"

"Holy shit!"

"Oh, mannn!"

Other comments flew through the air. One especially fat kid squeezed out of the first stall and tried to run out of the john; I stepped aside to avoid being flattened. Ray grabbed him as he went through the door.

All the way down the hall, with me in the lead and Ray following the herd from behind, I could overhear every form of bullshit from, "Hey, teacher, I wasn't smoking" to "My old man's gonna kill me" and "That was sneaky" to "That ain't fair, man."

We got them lined up all along the wall, all sixteen of them, while I went in to get the referral forms. When I came back out, Ray came over by me.

"Hey, none of us were smokin', man," one really grubby redneck insisted.

"Yeah, we'll all swear none of us were. Come on, Mr. C., we weren't smokin'!" one who knew, or had, Ray said.

I winked at Ray.

"Okay, okay, so none of you guys in those two bathroom stalls were smoking, is that it?" I asked.

They all nodded vigorously.

I looked at Ray and saw how badly he was trying to hold the laughter in, although he didn't know exactly what I was going to do.

"Okay," I continued. "So you weren't smoking, but you're not gonna insult my intelligence an' try to tell me you weren't all crammed into those two, small stalls, are you?!"

Well, they didn't really know how to answer that, until a handful said "no."

"Okay, okay, so we've established that you were *not* smoking but you *were* all in those two stalls. Hmmm, let's see...none of you were peeing because your little winkies were still inside your jeans...obviously none of you were sitting down on the toilets...so...." I said, pausing for the proper effect. I think Ray, by this time, might've been getting an inkling of what I was going to do...or say.

"Okay, Mr. Celetano," I began, turning to Ray, "so they weren't doing Number One…since nobody was peeing—"

"And they weren't doin' Number Two, 'cause no one was dumping," Ray added, "so…"

"So, fellas, all we can assume is that you were *all* in those stalls…doing Number *Three*!" I announced.

There was a brief silence of about ten seconds as the morons looked at one another in confusion, until one genius finally asked, "Number Three? What's Number *Three*?"

"Why, homosexual activity, of course!" I told him.

Well, you would've sworn I'd told them all they were going to be executed by firing squad in an hour. You see, at MVHS, suspensions are listed on the attendance sheet—that everyone has access to—with the name of the suspended student, and after the name, the violation. That got into their minimal brains really fast.

"But ain't that what it's gonna say on the suspension list?" another genius asked.

"Yup!" Ray and I said at the exact same time.

"Oh, shit, man, I don' want that!" I heard one guy say to another.

Their momentary confusion and consternation lasted a good half-minute before Ray winked at me and then said to them, "Well, if you guys don't wanna be written up for homosexual activity—which might put a little hurt on your chances of getting a prom date next month—Mr. Finn and I'd be willing to just write you up for smoking."

It took them about two seconds to agree to that. I had them each fill out their own referral, then Ray and I signed half each and Ray took them over to the vocational wing to Hartley, since I was now already five minutes late for my third-period class.

The next morning, both of us found, in our mailboxes, an actual form that said "COMMENDATION" in scrolled letters on top, with the following typed under it:

> For action on duty assignment in the spirit of professionalism, Mr. _____ is commended for

his dedication to his duty assignment. In school history, I am not aware of any teacher who apprehended sixteen individual students in violation of school rules at one time. Congradulations! Your are a asset to our school.
                      Signed,
                      A.H.T. Hartley
                      Asst. Principal

"Hey, Tom, *your* are *a* asset to our school!" Ray said as he walked into my room that morning before school began, waving his certificate.

"Be nice if he found out how to spell *congratulations*, too," I chuckled. "And why'd he put that *t* before *principal* at the bottom?"

"Whaddaya expect from a guy who spent a whole five years in the classroom?" Ray said.

"Yeah, as a goddam shop teacher!" I added.

The next day, Ray went to Wal-Mart and picked up two frames for us; we hung the commendations—upside down—in our rooms. They're still there.

17

"Where we goin'?" she asked me after coffee that Saturday.

"Well, I was goin' to Food Lion for tonight's dinner; you just decided to tag along."

"You don't want me to come? Whaddaya got, a hot cashier you're havin' an affair with?" she asked with a mischievous gleam in those blue eyes.

"Yeah, Daisy Loo and I go into the back and hump on the boxes of toilet tissue, just to be romantic. Anyway, I always do the food shopping on Saturday mornings, so this is somethin' you oughta be used to by now. You're usually vacuuming and doin' the laundry at your mom's."

"Too nice to be indoors this morning; we didn't do anything to get the cabin all that dirty; I'll do a quick run with the vacuum when we get back. So, what's for dinner?"

"I was gonna make stuffed pork chops…fried potatoes with scallions, and you can make some green beans up Southern-style with the bacon an' stuff like you did last time you felt like getting off your sweet ass to cook."

"Hey, you're the chef, hon! I can't hold a candle to the way you cook…an' anyway, I love the fact that you *do* cook, an' for *us*. More of what's romantic about you."

We'd bought the rest of the items on our list, and for April, we were able to find some decent-looking cherry tomatoes, so we decided on a salad as well. She'd never had the kind of potatoes I was going to make.

"Why scallions? Can't ya just use onions?" she asked.

"Yeah, but the flavor's not the same. You tell me what you think when you try 'em, okay?"

"What're you gonna stuff the pork chops with?" she wanted to know.

"You'll see, 'cause you're gonna be my assistant."

"Oh, boy, oh, boy! I'm gonna be an ass-istant!" she sang sarcastically.

"You are if you want a delicious dinner; otherwise, you can have the leftover horseshit and splinters again!" I growled.

When we got back, I got started on the stuffing.

"Okay, mince that onion and the tops of the scallions really fine an' put it all in that bowl. Then take that Granny Smith and do the same; everything's gotta be chopped really fine, okay?"

"Yes, dear. Would you like a beer while you're slaving over the stove?" she asked.

"What time is it?"

"Uhh...eleven-thirty."

"Well, it's after noon somewhere in the world. Yeah, gimme a Rock," I told her as I took the three red Serrano peppers over to the sink. I slit each one under cold running water, pushing the seeds out with my thumbnail.

"If you ever work with hot peppers, this is what you do," I told her as she put the green frosty bottle down to my right.

"Why?"

"The peppers have oil in them an' the water helps rinse some of it off, but don't be fooled: you gotta make sure you wash your hands thoroughly with soap and *hot* water...and don't put your fingers anywhere near your eyes, your mouth, or your nose, even after you've washed. An' something else about hot peppers—the smaller they are, the nastier they are."

"Okay."

While she was finishing with the onions and apple, I minced the chilis and a clove of garlic. Then I cut a tube of hot country sausage in half and dumped one half into the large, well-seasoned, black cast-iron skillet. After I'd fried that up, I dumped in the rest of the ingredients in the bowl, plus a tablespoon of Cajun seasoning, a teaspoon of Dijon mustard, and a pinch of dried thyme. Once everything was browned, I used a rubber spatula to scrap the pan into the bowl, adding a half-cup of bread crumbs and a cup of chicken broth. Mixing it all together, and then adding more crumbs until the mix was wet but not soggy, I covered the whole bowl in plastic wrap and put it in the refrigerator.

"We put the whole thing together about an hour before we wanna eat, maybe around four, how's that?" I asked her.

She just came up and hugged me, burying her face in my chest.

"I love you so goddam much! Sometimes I doubt that you exist, but you're always here, either waiting for me or comin' home to me. Where did you come from, anyway?" she sighed, squeezing me hard.

"I was born twenty-six years ago…and sent to you. It just took me twenty-five years to get here. Let's take a walk," I said, opening the door while she slowly and reluctantly unclasped her arms and followed me out into the backyard sunlight.

We stayed up really late that Saturday night and into the morning, sitting out on the first really warm-enough spring night. We'd talk for a while, then remain silent for a few minutes. I'd just listen to the early peepers or the first crickets. It was breezy that night, and the wind carried the distant sounds of the sparse traffic down below us on 211 or a hound off somewhere. She'd reach her hand out once in a while and take mine; for a while, she sat in my lap until we wanted beers; when I came back out, she was back in the other chair. When it got later, I'd gone in to get a couple old army blankets to keep the damp chill off us.

We talked…a lot. About whether she was sure she really wanted to give teaching a shot…or if it was just because she hoped maybe a position would open up at MVHS and we could be together, even at work…or if it was only because we'd both have the summers off.

"When did you *really* know you wanted to teach?" she asked.

"First day I actually got up in front of a class full of non-academic-minded kids and found out that first, I could hold their attention, and second, that I wouldn't turn into a huge puddle of nervous perspiration...and by the end of that day, I knew I'd found my niche, what I'd been destined...or chosen...to do. I found out I liked it."

"It had to help that you were considerably older than the normal college senior."

"I'm sure of it. If I hadn't spent the time with the Air Farce, I probably wouldn't have been any more mature than the kids I was supposed to be teaching," I told her. "I did a lot of growing up in those four years."

She thought about what I'd said to begin with.

"So I'm not really gonna be sure until I test the waters, huh?" she asked.

"I don't think so. College isn't really preparing you for actually doing it; in fact, I taught for less than a week when I realized that I could toss ninety-nine percent of what I'd been taught in education and psych classes right out the door."

"See, that's what I'm worried about, too. Most of the ed. classes I'm taking are taught by profs who haven't been in a real classroom for years! None of them would have the patience to deal with a Ronnie or some of the other kids you talk about. It's all theory and methodology bullshit!" she grumbled.

"Well, you're gonna find out this fall, and if you don't like it, there's other stuff you can do, I'm sure," I said, trying to ease her concerns but hoping she'd like it. She didn't ask me what 'other stuff' I meant and I was glad; I couldn't have thought of anything.

The conversation drifted off to other topics...or more quiet moments. We hadn't realized how late it had gotten until she'd gone in to get me another beer.

"Hey, sweet man, you know what time it is?" she asked, sticking her head back out.

"No."

"Try almost two; think we oughta call it a night?"

"Well, we better call it a morning, if it's after midnight," I said, standing up and stretching.

"Always a smart-ass comment...I don't know, maybe I'm makin' a mistake about you," she said as she closed the screen door and left the kitchen. I knew she was kidding but even the thought of not having her in my life gave me a momentary kick in the stomach.

We slept like spoons, leaving the windows slightly open to let in the almost-cold night air.

The banging on the door had me partly awake; I got up to pull on my shorts. Seconds later, Ronnie's voice came through the open window behind me, just as the shorts covered me.

"Hey, you two! Whatterya gonna do, sleep all day?! Hey, wake up! Big news!!"

I looked at the clock; it was just after ten, and we had slept at least two hours later on a Sunday than we usually did. Normally, we would've been down with Becky and Pop...and Ronnie for the usual huge country breakfast, but they had gone up to Woodstock for the weekend.

"What *is* that??!" Sandi groaned behind me as I went out into the little living room.

"The little blond demon, better known as your sister! This better be good!" I said.

"This better be goo—" I started to say as I opened the door, but Ronnie burst past me into the bedroom, just as Sandi disappeared into the bathroom.

Plopping her little ass down on our bed, she sat there with this inane...or maybe insane...grin, looking very pleased and excited about something.

"Well?!" I growled.

"When Sis comes out. Gotta tell both of ya," she replied smugly.

"Fine," I growled some more, heading for the kitchen to get the coffee going. I had just hit the brew button when the two of them appeared.

"So what is so important that you decided to ruin our beauty sleep?" I asked as she now plopped the same rear-end onto one of the kitchen chairs.

"The beauty sleep ain't workin' for you…and I know who the girl is!" she announced.

"What girl?" Sandi asked with a huge yawn.

"The girl who said Coach Jorgensen played with her titties!"

"How do you know?" I asked, suddenly very attentive.

"Rachel just called me on her cell…she goes to the Methodist church that has nine o'clock services an' before church started, she had to go to the bathroom…number two…an' she was in the stall when the girl's mother came in with another lady an' Rachel heard the whole conversation…all about the lawyer and what her daughter said. It's April Mitchell. Remember her?" she asked, looking at Sandi.

"Wasn't she a friend of yours, like all the way up to eighth grade or something?"

"Yeah, until she got boyfriends and we all just became nobodies. That's the one!"

"I guess I don't know her," I muttered.

"Naah, she takes all general and vocational classes. But Rachel has the Principles of Living class with her. She's one o' the ones I always mean when I talk about the ones who just wanna get married as soon as they can…but she's been drooling all over Coach since the beginning of the year; at least, that's what I've heard."

"Okay, so now we know who it is. So what?" I asked her.

I guess Ronnie hadn't taken it that far. It didn't take her long to get going again, though.

"I got a great idea! If we can get her to talk about it…an' record it…we got her good, don't we?!!" she practically shouted. "An' you got one of those voice-activated little recorders, T., so…I gotta go. Gonna call Rache back an' see what we can figure out!"

Before any words could come out of my mouth, she had flung the back door open and was gone.

"Now I know how the coyote feels when the road runner takes off!" I muttered.

It was *all* going to get very interesting, very soon.

18

It's funny, sometimes, how coincidence can play a role in our little lives.

Several weeks passed, with spring break looming. Easter came late that year and the kids—and most of the teachers—were getting antsy and ready for a break. Before it came, though, I finally had to ask Mark Battaglia about his sister.

When he came into fifth one day, as he passed my desk, I quietly asked him to stop to talk at the end of class. Of course, like most kids, when a teacher says something like that, they immediately think they're in trouble or something bad. When I saw him raise his eyebrows, I assured him that there was nothing wrong.

"Just need to ask you something," I said. He nodded and went to sit behind Ronnie, with whom a little more than a casual acquaintance seemed to have been slowly developing. I'd observed, in the past few weeks, their ritual, almost, of getting to class early to have a few minutes to talk. Ronnie would be positively energized as she chattered away or listened to him. Once, she'd turned back around when I'd begun class and had given me a large wink.

"So, you got something goin' with Mark, Slim?" I asked her that afternoon on the drive home. I guess she was so caught up in whatever was happening with them that she didn't even yell at me for what I'd called her.

"Oh, T., he's so mature! Not like these boneheaded dopes around here. I never thought I'd like someone from New York—"

"He's from Jersey, not New York," I said.

"Yeah, yeah, but from what he said, it was just across the river from New York City. Anyway, it's so easy to talk to him. He listens, and when he says something, it's intelligent. Like today, he was telling me that he thought I was ready for college an' needed to get outta here."

"So, because he agrees with you—and the rest of us—that makes him intelligent?"

"No! I don' know, I don' remember everything we've talked about, but when I talk to him on the phone—"

"Ah-ha!" I interrupted.

"Oh, shut up! Like you never talked to a girl on the phone in high school, right?!" she snapped.

"Oh, sure, I remember those conversations well: *'Well?...Well what?"...Say something...something...oh, that was real funny...don't you love me anymore?...you hang up first...gimme a kiss, I'*—ouch! Hey, stupid, I'm driving!" I yelped, rubbing my right ribs.

"Then shut up! We don't have dumb conversations like that! We talk about what we wanna do with our lives, important stuff like that!"

"Okay, okay, fine. But what are you gonna do next year if you get that letter next week from Tech an' he gets his? He hasn't applied anywhere close to Tech; the closest is William and Mary, I think."

"Well, considering the fact that we haven't even gone out or anything, I wouldn't worry too much about that right now…but God, I wish he'd make some kinda move!" she sighed, leaning back against the seat.

"You might have to make the first move," I suggested. "Since when have you lost your basic aggressive assertiveness?"

"It's different when you're…when you think you feel something for a guy. I can't just come up to him and say 'Hey, you wanna go out?'"

"Why not? Or maybe talk to Mom an' see if he wants to come to breakfast one Sunday," I suggested.

"What?! With *you* there, his teacher?!"

"I'm not his teacher on the weekends, Ronnie."

"Oh, shit, you're a teacher seven damn days o' the week! You *never* stop teachin' an' you know it!"

"Fine. Just make a move or it's gonna be August an' you'll be off to Blacksburg."

"You really think I'll get in?" she asked with concern and worry on her thin face.

"Yeah, sure; between your GPA, your SAT's, an' my wonderful letter, full of exaggerated lies, you're a shoo-in."

"Lies?!"

"Just kiddin', Slim," I said, slowing down as we entered Luray's town limits.

"Don't call me that!!"

"You wanted to talk to me?" Mark asked at the end of that class that day.

"Yeah...I'm just concerned, I guess. I'm sure you know what happened with M.D. and me, right?"

He grimaced and then nodded.

"An' it's none of my business anymore, I guess...but where is she?" I asked.

He seemed rather shocked that I didn't know.

"They just put her in another English class, that's all," he told me.

"You mean she's back in school?! Since when?"

"Like the week after my folks had to come into school. She's got that weird lady for English."

"You mean Miss Dunbar?!" I gasped, trying to visualize M.D. in that particular classroom.

"Yeah, that's the one, the one who talks to ghosts or somethin'. It's all she talks about at home."

"Is she okay?" I asked.

He shrugged.

"I guess. As okay as M.D. is ever gonna be. She's really mixed up, Mr. Finn. One day, she thinks she's a sex goddess, the next day she wants to change her image to Miss Goody...I don' know. I'd think it's something she shoulda got over...like, when she was thirteen, don'tcha think?"

It was my turn to shrug.

"Mark, I'm twenty-six and I don't think I understand women any better today than I did when I was ten!" I said with a chuckle.

He laughed.

"Well, you better wish me good luck, if that's true. I'm still tryin' to figure out your future sister-in-law," he admitted.

"So is the rest of the family, *and* her future brother-in-law. You gonna ask her out eventually?"

His eyebrows shot up again.

"You think she'd go out with me?!" he asked, a little surprised.

"Well, considering that most of the females in this school would like to, I'd say it's a safe bet. Just offer to drive her home after school or go for a soda or something. That'd give me a break from listenin' to her all the way home."

He laughed again; I liked his laugh.

"Yeah, we'll see. Well, I better get to sixth. See ya. I'll tell M.D. you were askin' about her," he said as he headed for the door.

"No!! Please do NOT do that!" I told him.

"Oh! Oh, yeah, not a good idea. Sorry, I wasn't thinkin'. See ya."

Two days after spring break, during which Sandi and I had taken a three-day escape to Virginia Beach to feed seagulls from our fifth-floor balcony and take late-night and early-sunrise walks on the long but narrow beachfront, it all hit the fan.

Mabel Dunbar had been part of the way into her third-period class and had stopped whatever she had been doing and had abruptly told her students to hand in their research papers. From what we heard, it had gone something like:

"What research papers?" some student had asked.

"Don't be insolent with me! You know very well what papers! Now pass them in!" Miss Dunbar had demanded.

Well, evidently no papers had been assigned, so the students had had nothing to hand in. When no one made a move at passing in a paper, Mabel had begun shrieking at them about being disrespectful and irresponsible, among other things.

"Jesus, lady, you're one friggin' whacko!" M.D. had told her and had gotten up, grabbed her books and her purse, and had headed for the door. When she had been about halfway there, Mabel had practically flown across the front of the room and had grabbed M.D. by an arm. Books went flying; then M.D. had given Dunbar a full, open-handed slap across her bony face, knocking her to the floor.

Still on the floor, Mabel had actually tackled the girl, dragging her to the floor with her, and then had stood back up, grabbing M.D. by her long, brown hair. With M.D. screaming from the pain and the rest of the class either sitting there, stunned or yelling, Paul Morgan, the English department chairman whose room was next door, heard all the commotion and had dashed next door, just in time to see Mabel trying to push M.D. out an open window.

"Paul said that the girl was kickin' and thrashin' at Dunbar and that Dunbar had kept screaming at her, calling her Clara and saying she had to die!" Deb told us at lunch.

"What were the rest of the kids in the class doin', just standin' there?" I asked.

"No. Paul said two guys had their arms around Mabel but she wouldn't let M.D.'s hair go. Finally one of the girls in the class dug her nails into one of Mabel's arms and she hadda let go, enough for Paul and the boys to break her hold on the girl!"

"Jesus Christ, what a basket case!" Wild Bill had observed. "But who woulda thought she'd freak out like that?"

"It doesn't surprise me. It's just like part of a long line of crazy stuff she's supposed to have done," Irene said. "Guess she just reached the end of her rope—"

"Yeah, and it snapped," I finished for her.

"So what happened then?" Bill asked.

"They called Hartley and Don from the phone in the room an' they came up with Officer Dean and took Mabel away. I heard she was still screamin' and moanin' about Clara and her mother and babblin' about all sorts of things," Deb added.

"What about M.D.?" I'd asked.

"A whole clump of her hair had been yanked outta her head. They took her down to the nurse, and I heard they rushed her down to Harrisonburg after that," Deb told us.

"For the hair?" Bill asked.

"I guess. Maybe they were gonna try to stick it back on or somethin' so she wouldn't have a bald spot or somethin'," Deb replied with a shrug.

"Her old man is gonna be a little pissed, I think," I suggested.

"Things just keep happenin' to that kid, don't they?" Ray asked.

"Yeah," Irene and I said together.

That was Mabel Dunbar's last day at MVHS, and, I would guess, her last year as a teacher anywhere. We got word sometime before the end of the school year that she was still in Western State, put there by an aunt, since Clara, we assumed, wanted nothing to do with the whole thing, if Clara was even still alive or aware of Mabel's problems. They hired a full-time sub to cover Dunbar's classes for the last month or so of the year.

That's not what I meant about coincidence, though.

19

Three weeks after that, Sandi was hired to fill the empty position for the next school year. The county school board pretty much had an unwritten rule that they'd hire their own graduates, as long as they had equal qualifications to any other applicants. With her 3.9 GPA and letters from three of her former MVHS teachers and two professors, Don called her at the cabin late one afternoon a day or two after her second interview to tell her she had the job. I think her upcoming marriage to me and the fact that I'd gotten a lot of respect in the first year there might have helped, although I'd rather think she got it all just for what she's bringing to the position. The superintendent, along with the education department at JMU, was going to consider her first three months at MVHS in the fall as the required student-teaching; she'd be issued a provisional teaching certificate until she'd finished up.

Speaking of our marriage, we'd talked about that with Pop and Becky; they'd been a little disappointed that we weren't going the church route, but realized that, ultimately, it was up to us.

On June 5, the Saturday after school had ended, very early that year because we'd started before Labor Day and had only one snow day, we replicated Pop and Becky's marriage, only with him being my best man and Ronnie the maid-of-honor. Needless to say, Ronnie cried through the whole twenty-minute ceremony. We'd held it outside, between the garden and our cabin, an assortment of lawn chairs set up for the guests. Pop had made a small trellis, I'd guess you'd call it, and a local florist had decorated it with all sorts of dried wildflowers. Sandi hadn't wanted roses; she said they were too expensive and died too quickly.

"Anyway," she'd said, "we can keep the wildflowers after that an' they can always remind us of us." I'd liked that. Pop had liked it, too, but because my mom had always grown and dried wildflowers.

We'd written our own vows, which we'd kept short, and had added them to the traditional ones. The commissioner of marriages did his legal thing in about three minutes, graciously accepted my "donation" to him in the plain white envelope, and had then headed for the refreshments.

Of course, Ray and Jo had been there, as well as the whole Lunch Bunch, a few of Sandi's new friends from college, and about three dozen of my students that Ronnie had told could come. One of them had been Mark.

After the ceremony, he had come over, somewhat hesitantly, with a present in his hands, Ronnie walking next to him, whispering something. He shook his head at her and then came up to the two of us after some other well-wishers had moved away.

"Uhh, congratulations, and…uhh…this is from the Battaglia family," he said, handing the gift-wrapped box to Sandi. She handed it to Ronnie.

"What?" Ronnie asked.

"Could you put it on the table with the other presents?" Sandi asked.

"No, we want you two to open it now," Ronnie said. Mark interrupted before she could say anything else.

"No, *she* wants you to open it now. You can open it whenever you want," he said firmly, looking at Ronnie with a stern expression.

"Okay, okay, let's open it before Slim here nags the poor boy for the rest of this beautiful afternoon," I suggested.

"Don't call me—"

"An' shuddup if you want us to open it," I added. She shut up.

Sandi sat down at the small table on the back porch and delicately opened the wrapping paper with a nail. I've never been able to figure out how women can do that so easily, by the way.

Opening the box inside the paper, Sandi pulled out a white, embossed envelope containing a card addressed to "*Sandi and Tom.*" She read what the card company had printed and then the neatly added, "*May your years together be happy, healthy, and filled with the joy of being with one another.*" It was signed simply "The Battaglias." In the card had been a slip of cream-colored stationery; Sandi read that, then handed it to me.

Apologies would be too late and by this time, meaningless. Thank you for teaching our children and making the last part of Mark's final high-school experience one that he wanted to talk about *every* night. We hope you will use this. Congratulations on choosing to commit yourselves to one another.

Gerry and Marie Battaglia

Attached to the stationery was a larger sheet of paper, on which had been typed:

TO WHOM IT MAY CONCERN:

MR. AND MRS. TOM FINN HAVE EXCLUSIVE RIGHTS AND PRIVILEGES TO ALL FACILITIES AT BLUE RIDGE SKI RESORT, INCLUDING ANY NECESSARY EQUIPMENT. THEY ALSO ARE TO HAVE ALL MEALS AND ANY AND ALL BEVERAGES FREE OF CHARGE AT THE BLUE MOON CAFÉ OR MOUNTAIN CREST RESTAURANT. UNIT #17, RIDGETOP COMPLEX, IS PERMANENTLY RESERVED FOR THEIR USE.

It was signed by Gerald Battaglia and two other functionaries of the "Blue Ridge Resort Corporation, 34 Park Avenue, New York, New York."

I looked at her; she looked at me. I think we were more than a little overwhelmed. I guess Mark noticed it, too, because he cleared his throat and said, "It's my dad's way of saying sorry and thanks at the same time. That's what he told me to say…that, and that he didn't want you to say no. Oh, yeah, he just said that when you want to use the unit, you just hafta call the main office up there—once the resort's done in August—and tell them when you're comin'."

The other item in the gift-wrapped box was a Lennox china swan that I knew was expensive; Aunt Hildy had always bought my mom some piece of Lennox for Christmases and had always found some way of reminding everyone that "it wasn't cheap, to say the least."

Sandi let out a long breath and said, "Well, I think I'm going to have one long thank-you card to write! Whew!"

That response let Mark relax, and with a handshake and a hug for the bride—who was wearing Becky's wedding dress, by the way—he walked off with Ronnie, who was positively beaming with a smile so wide I thought she was going to split her face.

"Y'know, maybe mob connections aren't so bad," I whispered to Sandi.

"Shh!" was all she said.

That left the wedding night. I wanted it to be special, despite the fact that we'd been making love for half a year. It had to be. She said it was.

20

"It's crazy," she said, "but it feels so natural, too." Yeah. Her body beneath me, her delicate arms outstretched across the pillows...her small hands clenching and opening, each time she sucked in a sudden breath or made some contented sound with her throat. All of me asleep except my head.

It all came so naturally...I didn't have to think of what to do, or what she wanted me to do, of what her body wanted. My mouth, exchanging my body's moistness with hers...hers: hot, wet, sweet...not something I can describe. Her body beneath me, a hand touching my head...her body beneath me, then a small foot resting on my shoulder...the silkiness of her thighs against me...as I tried to make her float.

Silly of me...it was I who was floating. My mouth, my lips, my tongue...all moving with her as she rose and sank, rose and sank, her softness sometimes pressing, sometimes twisting...and I floated with her.

Her wetness pushing against my lips as I explored the depths of her, her essence washing over me...a small foot, again, resting on my shoulder. As if I were a musician...her body the instrument...maybe a violin...each string sounding a sharp intake of her breath.

Making love to her a symphony, my only one...each rising breath, each tiny moan a crescendo in the symphony—my only masterpiece, only for her—

Following a romantic dinner, alone—two rare steaks, a bottle of old Cabernet, the crisp Greek salad—delicate looks in her blue eyes as she drank me in, a feeling of total and utter slavery to her if she wanted it...we enjoyed that dessert.

I made love to her twice...never stopping.

"What about you?" she whispered when her breath had returned.

"Later...or tomorrow."

"I want you to do that forever...I want to feel this way forever," she told me.

"I love you, you blond goddess," I whispered back.

"Oh, God...how can I ever want to get out of this bed?" she gasped with a tiny laugh as my lips touched her there, and there, and there...until she'd fallen asleep.

I got up quietly, and pulling on a pair of sweat pants, sat out back on the porch, the red flicker of the bug candle to keep me company, along with the katydids and crickets. I took a deep breath of the pine-scented air that also carried the early scents of late spring to reinforce how much I loved this particular place in Virginia. Somewhere off in the distance someone was coon hunting with his hounds. The stars, partially obscured by the full moon and scattered clouds, twinkled in their eternal journeys across the galaxy.

"What did I ever do to deserve this?" I asked Hank, my God. I took a long swallow of the cold Corona and closed my eyes. I'm sure I was smiling.

We put off anything like a honeymoon for a couple reasons—money, and the fact that we couldn't think of an affordable place to go that would have been any more beautiful than right where we were.

"We can maybe go somewhere during spring break next year," she suggested.

"If you want. But you might just wanna collapse and kick back by then, though. This year, I felt as if I were crawling toward that week off, that's how exhausted I felt. You'll know what I mean when you get there next spring."

"I'd rather take our honeymoon in little bits, anyway, I

think…like little weekend getaways or take a Friday or Monday off an' make it three days," she said.

"I like that idea," I told her. So we left it at that.

The school year had ended with a few things reaching some kind of closure.

M.D. had had her hair saved, although Mark told me that the doctors had told her that there'd be a thin, circular scar around the patch they'd been able to sew back onto her scalp. The Battaglias had shipped M.D. back north to relatives to try to make her happy, and, I suspect, to get her out of their hair, no pun intended.

Ida Mae Perkins, sued by the woman that Ida Mae had talked about in one of her classes, had resigned. None of us could figure out how she was going to pay off the settlement from the lawsuit without a job.

"Well, she's another one o' those whose family's been here since they started scalping Indians, so maybe the family has money. You know she's gotta be embarrassed to have her own dirty laundry hangin' out in public…an' especially in the school," Wild Bill commented.

"Yeah, there's a certain irony to her being the subject of all the gossip now," Irene said with a derisive laugh.

And Ronnie and Mark had both gotten into their first-choice colleges, with him going to William and Mary and Ronnie on her way to studying animals at Tech. They had hopes of maintaining a long-distance Virginia romance; in my mind, I wished them luck.

The summer went fast, way too fast. Sandi had gone back to her old job, working a forty-hour week at the 7-11, only to help out the owner, who'd had to let two of his employees go when he'd found out they'd been giving free food and drinks away to their high-school friends. Pop had decided that full retirement was too boring and had started his own landscaping business, very small to begin with. It got big really fast when Gerry Battaglia had seen "Finn's Landscaping and Trimming" either in the local weekly paper or the yellow pages and had called Pop to see if he wanted some business putting the plantings around all the unit complexes and four main buildings up at the ski resort.

With Sandi's help, Pop had found five guys who liked working outdoors rather than inside and had been willing to leave the retail world to work with him. Suddenly, he had three pickups and a whole load of equipment, all financed, temporarily, by the resort corporation—at very low interest. It seems that my experience with M.D.—but more likely with Mark—would never stop paying off. Oh, yeah, I was working for Pop, too.

Anyway, other than four Saturdays and two Sundays we'd had to work because there'd been too much rain during the week, I'd been able to start to plan out my second—and easier, I hoped—year of teaching. The six of us had gone hiking up along the Skyline Drive on two different weekends; *six* of us because Mark had come along to keep Ronnie breathing hard…she'd said it was from the hiking, but we knew better.

As for Pop, I was amazed by the changes in him since he'd come to stay back in the fall. If anything, he seemed to be getting younger. The lines of worry and the bags under his eyes were gone; the tan he always got so easily when I was a boy made him look rugged and fit, and being outside with his new vocation made it even deeper and darker. Between the youthful energy and love of Becky, and the absence of the agony of watching his wife—my mom—die slowly of cancer, Pop had become…I don't know…maybe just plain *happy* is good enough.

Sandi and I took a few day trips in Baby, just meandering along back roads, waiting to see what we'd find. We'd discovered a great place for lunch outside Keezletown and a few junk stores along Route 11, way up past Woodstock to rummage around in. We had started talking about a house, too.

"Whaddaya need a house for?" Becky had asked us as we lounged around the pool one Sunday afternoon.

"Yeah, what's wrong with the cabin?" Pop had added.

"There's not a lot of room for storage, for one thing, Pop," I'd told him.

"An' we really ought to be makin' our own lives, not livin' off Mom anymore," Sandi added.

Pop let out a long sigh.

"Well, I guess one bedroom ain't gonna be enough when kids start comin'," he observed. When I felt Sandi stiffen against me, I realized that I'd never told Pop he wasn't going to be a grandfather, ever. Becky's sudden sucking in of her breath alerted Pop to the situation, I think.

"Did I say somethin' wrong?!" he asked, looking concerned.

"I can't have kids, Pop, that's all," Sandi said softly. Ronnie had tears in her eyes.

He didn't say anything; neither did we…for a few seconds.

"Oh," was all he said. And that was it, pretty much.

"Anyway," I said, trying to get off the subject and erase it as well, "we're not in a hurry; as long as you're gonna charge us next-to-nothing rent for the cabin, we're planning on living on one of our salaries and banking the whole other one. I figure that within two or three years, we'll have enough and a good enough history of savings that we can put a down payment down on a piece of property and start buildin'."

"Up to you," Becky had said with a sad look of resignation; I guess she was already dreading her oldest moving away, especially since the other daughter was going to be five hours away come August. After all, Sandi had been able to commute to JMU, so Becky had had her girls with her always. I knew Pop would keep her occupied, though, and with the new Wal-Mart distribution center and the new computer-chip plant being constructed, I knew that the Alpine Motel would have some long-term renters for a while to keep Becky busy with customers, too. In early spring, she'd already filled three of the units with guys working on the ski resort, units that had been lying empty since I'd arrived a year before.

As I said, life was good. Wait, I just realized that I never said what happened with Jack Jorgensen.

21

It took halfway through July to reach closure on the situation that had pretty much sapped the spirit out of a guy so young. And if it hadn't been for Ronnie and two others, it might never have reached closure, at least, not the kind it did.

See, after Ronnie had discovered who the girl that accused Jack was, unbeknownst to the rest of us—at home or at school—she and Rachel…and Mark…had come up with a plan.

During the middle of May, Rachel had tested the April Mitchell waters by casually mentioning Mark's name on the way out of the Principles of Living class one afternoon.

"Oh, he's sooo hot!" April had reportedly gushed.

"I heard someone say he thought you were, too," Rachel had told her.

"*Really*?! He *really* did?!" she had asked excitedly.

"Yeah, but you don't have any classes with him, that's too bad," Rachel had said, all a part of the script she and Ronnie had concocted.

"But I eat on the same lunch shift as him!" April had said.

"That's where he's probably been lookin' at you. Well, then find some way to talk to him."

"Like what?"

"I don' know. I know he likes soccer an' Clint Eastwood movies, so maybe you can talk about that," Rachel suggested.

"But I don' know nothin' about soccer or Clint Eastwood," April had moaned.

Ronnie told us that she'd related all of this conversation with her fellow conspirators.

"I'll have to make the first move, I guess," Mark had said.

"Whatter ya gonna do?" Ronnie had asked.

"I don' know. Maybe I'll just watch to see when she takes her tray back an' get up at the same time an' offer to take it for her."

"Ooh, what a gentleman!" Rachel had snickered.

"Yeah, but that's what stupid April will prob'ly think, too," Ronnie had said. "Yeah, try that!"

Well, that had worked. Mark said that she'd handed him her tray but had walked along with him anyway, all the time making idle chatter and asking questions like did he like it here and what kind of car he drove.

"She was all flipped out when he said he had a Firebird," Ronnie had told us.

Well, the rest of the plan had been pretty easy, from what we were told. Mark had played her along for about a week or so, sitting with her by themselves as she'd ignored her usual friends at the lunch table they sat at. Eventually, Mark suggested a date.

"He took her over to New Market on Memorial Day to that movie theater an' then, on the way back, had just told her that he'd heard about her and the Coach."

"He just came out an' said something?!" Sandi had blurted out.

"Yeah, she was pretty shook up at first, Mark said, but he told her someone his mom knew had heard *her* mom tellin' someone about it an' I guess he made it sound cool enough that she didn't doubt it happened," Ronnie told us.

"Anyway," she continued, "at first, she didn't say anything more about it, but when he didn't say anything either, she asked him if it bothered him an' Mark said he didn't like girls who did stuff like that, an' especially with teachers or older men, and I guess she was afraid he wouldn't ask her out again, so she started talking about it an' wound up talkin' too much. So listen, okay?!"

Ronnie pressed the play button on my Sony recorder.

Over the sounds of the car and the radio or CD player, we could hear bits of April's voice.

"...I just told him....cute an' all....but he *laughed* at me!" she said angrily.

"He laughed at you?!" Mark's louder voice came off the tape.

"Yeah, an' it made me mad so I...him good....like I'm not some uggo or somethin'...an' Daddy got really mad (*it sounded as though a large truck came past Mark's car here because that's all we could hear on the tape*)....fix him good....his job....just don't like to be laughed at, ya know?"

"So he really didn't do anything to you?" Mark had asked...very clearly.

"No, but I don't do things like...so I'm not....kind of girl, either," she had replied.

The tape went on for another twenty minutes or so, but she dropped the topic of Jack Jorgensen and rambled on about nothing I'll bore you with.

I'd looked at Sandi and she looked at me. Ronnie was looking very pleased with herself...as she should have been.

I was waiting when Don Dempsey walked in the next day, the second-to-last day of school.

"More trouble?" he asked, the eyebrows raised again.

"Not this time...or at least, not for anyone that doesn't deserve it," I said, pulling the Sony out of my bookbag. "Got something you need to listen to."

By the end of the day, the vice-chairman of school board and the superintendent had received a written transcript of the tape. Don had Chuck make a copy of the tape as well.

It took the Mitchells' lawyer several weeks to stop stonewalling Jack's lawyer until a closed session took place at the school-board office. Besides the Mitchells and Jack and his lawyer, Mark Battaglia had also been asked to appear as a defense witness if necessary.

Once they'd heard the tape...and April had pretty much been shocked into admitting that she'd lied about the whole thing, Jack had received a lukewarm apology from the school-board members who'd been more willing to believe the girl's story; Don had apologized to Jack for what he had been through, as had the superintendent. Jack's lawyer informed the Mitchells that he would be counter-suing them for the emotional damage his daughter had done to Jack and Jack's reputation, as well as for Jack's legal expenses.

A month later, the whole thing was settled out of court; all we found out was that the settlement covered Jack's legal costs and more; we could only guess that the Mitchells' finances had been somewhat, if not significantly, further depleted.

I don't know about the emotional damage to Jack, but before he took a job in a neighboring county, he'd called me to say goodbye and tell me he was sorry he wouldn't be working with some of us anymore.

"I just can't stay here. Even if everyone is willing to believe I didn't do anything, I'll have to deal with the history of the same thing from now on. See you, Tom. Maybe I'll see you at a game next fall."

"I like it here at MVHS, Jack, but between you and me, I hope your kids kick some Fighting Black Bear butts, too," I told him.

He'd laughed and hung up.

The next fall, he took his new school's undefeated team to the state finals and was chosen Virginia Football Coach of the Year. Irony has its place.

The final pieces of the closure were Don's phone call to me and the dinner we took Ronnie, Rachel, and Mark out to at the Brookside.

"Hey, Tom, Dempsey here."

"Hi, Don, what's up?" I'd asked on that July afternoon.

"Just wonderin' about something. You gonna be involved in solving every mystery that's gonna happen here?!" he asked with a laugh.

"Huh?"

"Well, you figured out the Knopf thing, and now the Jack Jorgensen affair."

"Not me, Don. All I did was bring you the tape. My just-graduated sister-in-law has to get the credit for that…her and two other kids."

"Well, maybe next year you'll just be able to teach…although you mighta made a pretty decent detective, I guess," he said. "Anyway, I really called you just to congratulate you on the marriage. You sure kept it a big secret from the rest of us!"

"Well, my wife wanted to keep it small and quiet, and I didn't want the faculty to think they needed to get us a present or anything."

"Wish *my* wife had felt that way fifteen years ago! Oh, and by the way, I've run into a lot o' parents in town and in the county who've had nothing but good things to say about what their kids said about bein' in your classes…and when I was golfin' with Paul this past Saturday, he told me that he wishes he knew as much about teaching in his first year as you do."

"Thanks, Don…that means a lot to me, comin' from Paul."

"Guess that's why he didn't think he had to observe you more than twice. First-years are supposed to be observed a minimum of six times."

"Does that mean I've got a problem?" I asked, suddenly worried.

He laughed.

"Yeah, he might only observe you once next year. Hey, enjoy the rest of the summer. See you in August," he said, hanging up.

Oh, and one last thing: remember that commercial for "Nursery Boys"? Well, it seems that the boys weren't ready to do whatever they were supposed to have been working on and had delegated Eric to come ask me for an extension, or at least to allow them to do their filming the second day.

It seems that when Eric had finally, nervously, with great terror in his heart, approached me, I had smiled and told him, "Hey, you guys're goin' second, so get ready," which had completely blown his mind and sent him back to spread the bad news. With nothing else to do, they'd written that dumb jingle in about two minutes while the weird kid, Dan, had sneaked outside and had yanked that shrub out of the ground at the back of the school. Then they'd discovered that they all wore boxers and had worked up enough courage to appear in them and their T-shirts. I'm glad none of them wore jockey shorts, instead.

After all, I *have been* trying try to teach my kids to be creative and resourceful. I guess I have.

As I said, life is good…and seems to be getting better. But I could do without any more mysteries or major personal crises next year. As for normal crises, I'm in teaching, so they're never going away permanently, since the kids I teach will be changing every year. At least I'll have a beautiful blond goddess teaching alongside of me this time. And I am going to miss the skinny sister…and a lot of others.

Teaching…what a marvelous profession. Even with the stress.

And as my second—and Sandi's first—school year began, everything was going fine until that night around nine, sometime after Halloween that fall, when the two bulletholes appeared in the window at the back of the cabin.

22

Sandi had been down at the main house, doing Becky's hair, when it happened. I had just finished grading a batch of essays on the kitchen table, our humble abode not being big enough for a desk *and* a computer table. I'd just gotten up to stuff the papers into my bookbag by the front door so I wouldn't forget them the next morning when I heard the two muffled reports a split second after bits of glass were scattered across that same kitchen table. At first, I'd simply thought that some local along 211 had been out coon hunting again. I thought differently when I saw the glass bits reflecting on the table and saw the picture of Old Rag Mountain fall from the front wall of the cabin.

I hit the floor and crawled my way to the phone and dialed 911.

"Hello, Page County sheriff's office," a raspy female voice announced.

"I'm at the Alpine Motel, Route 211. Two bullets were just fired into my cabin!" I yelled, I'm sure.

"Name please?"

"Finn, Tom Finn, I'm in the large first cabin behind the motel office!"

"Dispatching a deputy right now, Mr. Finn. Please turn off all lights and do not expose yourself," her voice told me. I didn't bother to tell her that I had planned to do that...nor did I think of a witty comeback about "exposing myself." I was a little shaken.

I dialed Becky and Pop's number.

Sandi answered and then actually screamed when I told her.

"Shut up, I'm okay!" I told her. "Turn out your lights an' wait for the cops to arrive!"

She hung up; I crawled to the lamp on the small end table, shut it off, then slithered along the floor to the kitchen, and sliding up against the wall between that window and the door, reached up, turning off the kitchen light and turning on the outside porch light and the single floodlight mounted under the eaves, lighting up the back grass for thirty yards or so.

Nothing happened. I ducked down, crawled all the way into the dark bedroom and cautiously drew a small triangle of curtain aside and looked out. Nothing moved; the window was open about three inches; no sounds. No sounds of feet running away, no engines starting...not that there was any place for a vehicle to travel out back...unless it was a dirt bike or an ATV. Still, I heard nothing.

About five minutes later, the patrol car arrived.

The two deputies stopped at the office first, then crept slowly up to the cabin, high beams on and the spotlight on the passenger side swinging back and forth. I flicked the front outside light on and off.

They beeped the horn. Opening the door a crack, I shouted, "Nothing. You wanna come in?"

"Where'd the shots come from?" a voice yelled.

"Out back, two of them."

The one on the passenger side told me to go back inside and wait. They brought the car directly in front of the front door so that the car was totally shielded from the back; then they got out and knocked. I let them in and turned on the lamp on the end table. They carried those long black flashlights, still lit.

The first one in was in his forties somewhere, gray hair below the edge of the Canadian Mountie-style hat, a moderately prominent belly testing the strength of the wide leather belt; the other one couldn't have been more than twenty-three. He had the hat off, his hair cut military-style, and very intense eyes that told me he took his job seriously. In other words, he wasn't one of those local yahoos who just went into law enforcement to impress the rural dingbat women by wearing the big handgun in public.

The older one spoke first.

"You Mr. Finn?"

"Yeah."

"I remember you. You was the teacher who figgered out that kidnappin' thing, wasn't you?"

I didn't remember his being one of the police I'd talked to then, so I figured he'd just heard the name.

"Yeah. But I think I'd like you guys to figure this one out, okay? I'm very happy to leave the detective work to the pros this time," I said, trying to push some of the tension out of me. It was then that Sandi burst through the front door.

All three of us jumped.

"Ma'am, we asked you to stay at the office," the older guy, whose name I saw was "Wilkey" on the thin gold nameplate above his right breast pocket, said.

"I know, but that's too bad. This is my house and this is my husband, an' if it was okay for you to get into the house, it was okay for me!" she snapped, coming to me and wrapping her arms around my middle.

"It's okay, Fred. Let's check out the cabin. Sir, could you show us where the bullets entered? I think you can turn the lights on now," the younger one, who introduced himself as Deputy Siewert, asked in a soft, deliberate voice.

I turned on the kitchen light and pointed to the window and the glass-covered table.

"I think one of the shots hit a photo on the wall over there," I said, going back to the framed picture that was now on the floor; the glass had cracked diagonally from one corner of the frame to the other when it had hit the floor. In the middle of Old Rag Mountain was a neat hole.

Siewert came over to take the picture from me.

"Looks like a pretty large caliber, Fred," he said, holding the back up to the light.

The older one was already digging at a hole in the wall with a folding knife. I noticed a second hole about four inches to the right of the one he was working on.

"There's where the other one went," I said, pointing at the paneling.

Siewert went to work on that one.

In less than a minute, Wilkey had two shiny slugs in the palm of his hand.

"Jacketed, too. I'd say thirty-ought-six maybe," he muttered.

"Yeah, I think so," Siewert said, nodding. "Good thing you weren't in the line of fire, sir. These would've gone right through you if they hadn't hit bone...an' they coulda done some nasty work on the way through." He continued to stare down at the slightly blunted projectiles now in his palm.

"You got any idea who mighta done this, sir?" Wilkey asked.

"Not a clue. Far as I know, I don't have any enemies," I told him, starting to feel as if I were in a bad movie instead of standing in a motel cabin we called home.

"Maybe they were just stray shots?" Sandi asked hesitantly. I could tell she didn't believe that, but was hoping it was something as dangerously innocent as that.

"Well, ma'am, first of all, you can't use a rifle like this to hunt in the county, and I don't think anyone is out doin' target practice in the dark. I'm sorry to say it, but someone has some mean intentions toward your husband," Wilkey said.

I got that really lousy loose-bowels feeling right then.

"Maybe he just doesn't like cabins," I said, trying to be funny but when I'd said that, I realized that my mouth had suddenly gone very, very dry.

Both deputies frowned disapprovingly at my feeble attempt at humor.

"Mr. Finn, you need to be real careful for now. Stay away from windows, an' I'd recommend you git some curtains for those kitchen windows. Don't turn too many lights on, either," Wilkey instructed. "Cover the glass in that door, too."

Meanwhile, after peering out through the small back door,

Siewert opened it and went out, holding the flashlight in his left hand with the arm at a right angle to his body; Wilkey followed him.

"My God, what the hell is goin' on?!" Sandi gasped, a terrible look of helpless fear in her blue eyes.

I hugged her, as she squeezed me.

"I don' know. This is crazy. I don't have anyone I know mad enough to shoot me!"

She started to cry.

"Hey, it's okay!" I told her, holding her out in front of me.

"No, it's *not*!! How can you say that?! Someone shot a rifle at you, Tom!! It's *not* okay!" she yelled angrily now.

"Okay, okay, it's not okay, but don't go getting hysterical on me, all right?!"

She nodded, then sniffled a little and wiped at the tears with the back of her hand.

The deputies came back about five minutes later.

"Well, there's nothing we could see; too dark," Siewert announced. "We were hopin' maybe there'd be footmarks back there in the grass, but we couldn't see anything. We'll come back in the morning an' look around. Maybe we'll be lucky an' find the shell casings."

"We'll be able to figger out the angle them shots came into the cabin at an' have a good chance of at least findin' where the shooter was," Wilkey told me. "Don't do anything to those windows until we come back, all right? For now, I'd just call it a night an' try to git some sleep. Guess you got school tomorrow, doncha?"

"Yeah, we both do," I told him.

"Well, we'd better go. Got a report to write up. Like I said, we'll be back in the mornin'. Someone gonna be here?" he asked.

"Yeah, my mom'll be at the office," Sandi told him.

They nodded, told us they were sorry about our problem, and left.

Two minutes later, Pop and Becky burst through the front door. We didn't get much sleep that night.

23

I was just closing the door to my classroom that afternoon to grade some more papers during my fifth-period planning when Don Dempsey and an officer wearing double-silver captain's bars appeared at the same door.

"Tom, this is Captain Blake from the sheriff's office; he needs to talk to you. Everything okay?" Don asked, his large dark eyebrows raised in their usual way.

"Someone shot into our place last night," I told him, causing Don's eyebrows to go up to their maximum height. Even his eyes seemed to get larger behind the lenses of his metal-rimmed glasses.

"What?!"

"Yeah, don' know more about it. Guess that's why the captain is here, right?" I said, turning to the officer.

He was a tall man, maybe forty, like Wilkey, but unlike the deputy, muscular and trim; his uniform was neat, the trousers sharply creased. He had gray eyes a little too close together on either side of a long, thin nose. The gray moustache was all military; he held the Mountie hat in his hand. I guessed he had Marine Corps in his background. He wore no gun. I remembered him from the Knopf tragedy the year before. He'd been one of the detectives to question me.

"Nice to see you again, Mr. Finn...although I'm sorry about the circumstances. Mind if we sit?" he asked.

"No, pick anywhere," I said.

"Well, I better get back downstairs," Don said but I could tell he was dying to know what the newest mystery in my young life was…and hoping it wouldn't disrupt the normal routine of Mountain Valley High School. I was hoping it wouldn't disrupt the rest of my life…or end it.

Blake ran a hand through his thick hair and sighed.

"We haven't had anything like this happen around here for a couple dozen years," he informed me. "Any idea who might've done the shooting last night?"

I shook my head.

"We were out there a few hours ago. Took us about an hour to find where the shots came from. He was up that hill, bottom of the mountain, a couple yards above the treeline. No casings, sorry to say. He did leave five Marlboro butts behind, though."

"Is that good?"

"Could be, if we get some idea who it might be. Get a DNA sample and match it with the saliva on the cigarette filters. We get a match, we got the shooter. That's why I really need you to think of anything—and I mean *anything*—that you might've done to get someone this riled up." He leaned back and stared hard at me.

All I could do was shrug.

"Look, Captain Blake, we didn't get much sleep last night, as you could probably guess, so all we did—my wife and I—was try to figure that out."

"And?"

"Nothin'. I mean, the only conflicts I had all last year were a few kids who were unhappy with their grades. No parent conferences…well, I did have one."

"What about?"

"Oh, I had a teenage girl with the usual crush who took it a little too far an' told her parents I'd made advances…but that all got resolved. She broke down and admitted she'd lied."

"Maybe the parents are still angry, though," Blake conjectured.

I shook my head again.

"No, I don't think so. They gave us a really big wedding present which included free everything at Blue Ridge Resort."

It was his turn to raise eyebrows.

"The new ski place? Was the girl the daughter of the builder?"
"Yeah."
He just nodded. "I don't think Mr. Battaglia goes in for hiding in woods to shoot someone," he observed. "And he doesn't smoke."
"You know him?" I asked, surprised.
"Played golf with him a couple times a month ago or so, before they went back north. Nice enough guy…considering."
"So I assume you know who he is," I said cautiously.
"Let's just say I know *what* he is an' I know he wouldn't do anything like what happened to you last night. So let's get back to you. No other conflicts, arguments, any of that? With anyone?"
I could only shake my head.
"Okay, look, I'd like you to do this, then…when you feel up to it, but don't take too long. Make a list of all the things you've had your students do, last year an' so far this year. Then make a list of all the people you've come into contact with beyond the scope of your job…not including cashiers at Food Lion or Wal-Mart or anything normal like that. Understand what I mean?"
"Yeah, but what for?"
"Just do that for me, an' if there's anything I can figure out that might have caused the problem…that wouldn't occur to you, I'll tell you more. Otherwise, I won't waste your time. Remember, you said you wanted to let the pros do it," he added, making me aware that he'd either talked to the two deputies or they'd written a very detailed report.
I laughed a little nervously.
"Yeah, it's all yours…and I hope you solve it soon. My wife's a bundle of nerves because of this, an' my dad, who's a Vietnam vet, is growlin' about getting himself an M-16 and some camouflage!"
"Well, I hope he just stays growlin'. Last thing we need is someone playing commando out there," Blake said, giving me a questioning look.
"Oh, I think I can calm Pop down," I told him, "but the wife's another matter."
"Don't have to tell me. My wife's been a bundle of nerves for the

last twenty-some years, bein' married to a cop. Okay," he said, standing up and picking up his hat from the desk he'd been sitting at, "get back to me soon as you can. Here's my card—anytime, day or night. And stay away from the windows when it's dark."

I nodded and watched him leave. The loose-bowels feeling was still there.

Sandi and I brainstormed that night; we'd emailed Ronnie at Tech and asked her to do the same, not telling her exactly why I needed her to remember everything she'd done in both classes.

I'd gotten a similar schedule that year; I had one writing class, one senior and three junior classes, this time all accelerated. As a first-year rookie, Sandi had gotten only one prep, but they were all non-academic juniors; I'd asked Paul to give her two of my accelerated and me two of hers, but he'd shaken his head.

"Sorry, Tom...had a lot o' parents in over the summer to request their kids get you. That's what you get for doin' such a good job with the juniors last year. Sorry...politics, y'know," he'd explained. "Did the best for your missus with only one preparation. She'll be able to handle it. After all, you married her, so I don't have to tell you that she's no pushover. I don't think I'll have to worry about the usual first-year teacher's problem with classroom management."

I'd told him I thought he was right; still, I'd rather she'd gotten at least one or two of the easier classes. I was to find out that year that they could give Sandi tiger pups and she'd find a way to train them her way.

"Okay, whadda we got?" I asked her as she stared down at the legal pad of yellow lined paper.

"Grammar unit...Colonial period...family oral-history projects...weekly research papers...magazine logs...adolescent lit...commercials....umm...documentation...five movies...mini-scripts...writing process...that's it," she said, looking up at me.

I thought some more. "*What else? I must've done more than that!*" I thought to myself.

"Add drama unit…poetry and music…understanding how to interpret and analyze a poem…scavenger hunts—"

"Scavenger hunts?!" she asked with a frown.

"Yeah, just some fun competition stuff; I broke them into teams in the library and they hadda find the answers. First team to finish got pizza, the rest lesser stuff. They had a ball!" I told her.

"Those librarians musta loved it!" she said sarcastically. "How did you get them to let you do that?"

"Well, they don't like me but I think I intimidate them, too," I told her. "An' it's of educational value. If they'd told me I couldn't, they know I'd have gone to Don or Paul an' they would've had to."

"You know, neither of them were there when I was at MVHS. We had just one, Mrs. Cahill, and she would fall over herself tryin' to help us with our research or to pick out a good book. But these new ones, especially that Gaucher woman, she acts as though the damn library is hers, as though it's not part of the school."

"Funny, that thought has occurred to me…and most of the faculty. The only ones she gets along with are the few misfits that the rest of the staff can't stand. The kids call her 'Mrs. Hitler.' And they really resent the way she talks to them as if they're all still in elementary school. Anyway…oh, yeah, put down business-and-career unit, and…that's all I can think of. Maybe Ronnie'll have stuff I haven't thought of."

"Doncha still have lesson plans from last year?" she suggested.

"Oh, shit, sure! Hang on, lemme dig them—oh, shit, they're in the file cabinet at school. Well, this is plenty. Lemme email this to Blake an' let him try to squeeze some clues outta it," I said, taking the sheet of paper and going into the living room to the new Dell we'd purchased together.

I was just sitting down in front of it when the phone rang.

"Got it!" she called from the kitchen. "Hello? Yes, hold on. Hon, it's for you," she said, holding the wall phone out to me.

"Hello?" I asked as I put it to my ear.

"You got a fuckin' month to git yer sorry ass outta the county. You still here at Thanksgivin' an' I'll be stuffin' mah turkey with your sorry ass!" a harsh voice told me.

"Your turkey is gonna taste like shit then, asshole!" I said, hanging up. My hand was shaking.

Sandi stood there, the blue eyes wide with fear.

"Who was that?!" she gurgled.

"Our rifleman, I think," I told her, telling her the gist of the phone call.

"Quick, hit star 67!" she said.

"Huh?"

She snatched the phone out of my hand and punched some buttons on the phone. Then she frowned, held down the cradle and did it again.

"Shit!" she said, hanging up the phone.

"What was that all about?" I asked.

"I thought you were supposed to hit star and then 67 an' it'd tell you what the number that just called was. All I got was the dialtone again!"

I took a deep breath.

"Well, maybe I'd better call Blake instead of emailing him," I said as I took his card from under the magnet on the refrigerator and dialed his number.

24

"He said it's star *69* not 67," I told her as I hung up the phone.

"What else did he say?" Sandi asked.

"He said not to call it; they can find out where the call came from from the phone company. He seemed surprised we don't have caller ID; I guess most teachers have it, at least, that's what he implied. Anyway, you heard my end of the call. He just said he'd get going on it."

"Tom, I'm really really scared. Do you know how many guns there are in Page County…and how many rednecks with the IQ of a gnat have multiple ones?!"

"Yeah, I've seen the gunracks. It seems that sloping foreheads and full gun racks…along with Confederate flags…seem to go together, and by the sound of the guy's accent, he's in that group," I admitted. I also admitted that I was "concerned," too; she didn't need to hear *me* say "*scared.*" I was supposed to be the strong veteran; I wasn't feeling that way at the time. Fortunately, our jobs gave us a chance to keep our minds off the current crisis, at least until three-thirty or so. We got a well-needed dose of comic relief the following morning.

In the past month or so, we had established the Breakfast Club, which contained all the members of the Lunch Bunch, although Ray sometimes didn't make it. We'd kidded him about the honeymoon being "over," to which he'd replied, "When the honeymoon's over, so is everything else." I knew what he meant, but he'd learn he was wrong about that.

Anyway, our Breakfast Club also contained about a dozen of our students, some whom we shared, some that just belonged to one of us. Of mine, there was a handful from a very special moment in that second year, some of whom had spilled over from the previous year.

The comic relief that morning came from my old buddy Joe, who'd come to me that previous fall to ask whether I thought he could get away with killing and burying his thought-to-be-pregnant-but-wasn't girlfriend. If I were a psychiatrist, I'd probably have strong suspicions that more than one person was inside Joe's mind.

You see, he was a very destructive young man; he delighted in smashing things with the sledgehammer he kept in the trunk of his totally mint '73 GTO and had been put on juvenile probation for turning two public-park benches into toothpicks, just because he'd gotten mad at his father. On another occasion, he'd reduced his neighbor's prefabricated aluminum outbuilding to the height of about three feet by repeatedly hitting it with a bowling ball he'd swiped from an alley in Harrisonburg, a ball he'd attached about three or four feet of steel cable to.

On the other hand, his craftsmanship and skill with carpentry were unbelievable for someone his age. The previous spring, he'd taken me down to fourth-year wood shop (which he was already taking, despite being a junior) to show me the cherry hutch he'd built for his mother for Mother's Day.

"Never seen anything like this kid," Mr. Craig, the teacher told me. "Cherry wood's real expensive an' he never made a mistake. He handturned those legs, did all the scrollwork and curves by hand, and hand-sanded it. Put five or six coats of varnish on it—varnish, not polyurethane. That thing'd cost a few thousand in a furniture shop, at least, an' it still wouldn't be that good. The kid's a damn genius, I think."

Joe had just stood there, beaming.

"Pretty good, huh, Mr. F.? You want me to make something for you?" Joe asked.

"Just stay outta trouble, Joe, that's what you can do for me," I told him.

"Pfff!" he said, rolling his eyes. "Ask for something that's possible!" he said with a manic laugh. Anyway, that's Joe. Oh, I meant to mention that over the summer, he'd picked up a sidekick named Joel.

I referred to Joel as Joe's "henchman," since he seemed to have fallen into the role of carrying out Joe's plans and getting Joe the necessary materials. It had been Joel who'd found enough M-80's for Joe to put together the pipe bomb that they'd used to blow up the old, abandoned water tower that had been ruining Joe's view of the mountains from where he lived. Only a couple of us knew about that, by the way.

Anyway, that morning, most of the breakfast gang were munching on the assorted stuff we contributed to the general appetite when I heard this insane laughing and loud voices coming down the hall toward my room. I could pick up snatches of the conversation, kind of like listening to the tape that Mark had made of April Mitchell.

"...no, I tell 'im....come on, you always....my car, wasn't it?....sure you tell *all* of it!"

That much we heard before Joe and Joel, owner of an unruly mop of brown hair that looked like a wild bush, more or less burst—in what might have been taken as drunken stumbling but wasn't—into the room.

"I say, what seems to be going on?" Wild Bill said in a Monty Python accent.

"Lemme tell 'em, lemme me tell 'em!" Joel said to Joe.

"No. I tol' you already! I did it, so I tell 'em!" he growled.

"Okay, okay, but you leave anythin' out an' I tell 'em the rest!" Joel argued.

"Yeah, yeah, fine. Hey, Mr. F., what's happenin'?" Joe said as if we hadn't heard the previous part of the dialogue.

"So, Joe, what's to tell?" I asked.

"Yeah, Joe, an' so early in the morning?" Irene added through her bagel.

"Okay, well, you know my car, right?" he said, looking at me.

"Well," I said, still trying to be the English teacher, "I don't personally *know* the car but I assume you mean do I know about that cherry GTO, right?"

"Yeah, yeah. Well, we decided to go cruisin' a little last night, y'know, an'—"

"We went all the way over the mountains to I-81!" Joel said, interrupting.

"I said *I'm* telling the story!" Joe growled some more. Joel shut up.

"Okay, so we're over on I-81, an' it's maybe eleven o'cloc—"

"It was twelve-thirty!" Joel said.

"Shuddup. So it's after midnight an' there ain't much traffic where we were so I put the ol' pedal to the metal and buried the needle on the speedometer..."

"It goes all the way up to one-twenty!" Joel gurgled moronically.

Joe just gave him a look this time that clamped Joel's lips shut again.

"Okay, okay, so I got it up to that an' I look in the rearview mirror an' there ain't nothin' comin' behind me, no lights or anything, an' only a couple sets o' headlights on the other side, goin' down towards Harrisonburg, you know, an'—"

"Would you tell them already?! Jeez-us!" Joel yelled.

"So I got it up to top speed annnddd..." he said, pausing for effect, I assumed, "an' I—"

"He threw the goddam thing in *reverse*!!" Joel yelled. Joe hopped up from the desk chair he'd been sitting in and hit Joel on top of the head with a closed fist.

While Joel was rubbing the top of his head, Joe turned to us, and with the same kind of proud, beaming smile that he'd had when he'd shown me the cherry hutch, just nodded and said, "Yup!!"

"Yeah, man, you shoulda seen it!" Joel began to shout. "There was automatic trans fluid all over the place, an'—"

"We did at least four or five three-sixties an' you could hear pieces of the trans clinkin' and flyin' all over the place. We wound up in the grass in the middle o' the interstate. Man, what a pisser!" Joe said with another maniacal laugh.

"You blew up that classic car, you idiot?!" Wild Bill, a great lover of great cars, yelled at them.

"Naah, we didn't blow up the car. The car's okay, just gotta get a new trans, that's all," Joe said very calmly. "My mama's getting it towed home this morning."

"But what in the world did you want to do that for?" Deb asked after she'd gotten over the shock.

"Just wanted to see what would happen," Joe replied matter-of-factly with a shrug.

"Man, there was trans fluid all *over* the goddam place!" Joel repeated with that inane smile on his goofy face.

"Well, we gotta go get some breakfast at Hardee's," Joe said, "Guess we're gonna miss first period again. See y'all." And they left.

Nothing bad happened in the next few days. I got a visit from Blake that Thursday afternoon, after school.

25

"Sorry I took a little long to get back to you, but I figured that since we hadn't heard from you, nothing new had happened. The phone call you got came from a pay phone in that shopping center on the west side of Luray, so no luck there. It's the list of things you did with your classes that I'm a little more interested in," he told me, pulling a sheet of paper out of a thin leather zippered folder he'd brought with him.

"The only ones I've got questions about for now are…let's see…documentation? What's that about?"

I told him what it was—teaching the kids to use footnotes and make works-cited pages to avoid charges of plagiarism.

"No, don't think that's it….adolescent lit?"

"Just taught them some general stuff about adolescent psychology and then we read *Huck Finn* and *A Separate Peace* an' I had them apply what they knew about themselves and the psych to our discussions of the novels."

He thought for a minute.

"I'm assuming that your friend in the woods is an adult, an' the line I'm workin' on is that something you might've done in class got talked about at home an' maybe some narrow-minded parent capable of violence took exception to it. Ring a bell?" he asked, one eyebrow higher than the other.

I thought about what I'd done with the students.

"Well, I gave them some typical teenage problems and asked them to discuss what the kids in the scenarios could do, what choices they had."

"Example?"

"Well, you know, like if their parents were abusive, if they had a friend using drugs or a girl friend who was giving away sex to keep a boy, if they had a father who was never happy with anything they did…stuff like that."

"In other words, typical situations. Did any of your students seem to get emotionally rattled when you discussed any of those, like maybe the situation was too close to home?" he wondered.

I couldn't think of any. I told him that some had admitted to knowing "friends" with those kinds of problems; a few had admitted to experiencing something like them.

"But I don't recall any that seemed to set off alarms, and I'm pretty good, I think, at noticing all my kids and what their reactions are."

He nodded.

"All right. What's the family oral-history project all about?"

That set off an alarm…only because of what he'd asked me to concentrate on. First, I told him what the project was about and why I'd had my students do it.

"Okay, you know what oral history is, I assume, so I won't bother explaining that. When I came down here, what with all the history around us and the fact that a lot of these kids have families that go back a hundred years or more in the same place, I thought it'd be good to have them research their own family histories instead of just doin' the usual research paper."

"What did they have to do?" Blake asked, beginning to look interested.

"Well, first they had to tape interviews with at least four relatives, and they had to have at least two of them from different generations…like they could do their parents, but they'd have to interview grandparents, an' if they were all dead, great-aunts or uncles. They could do more than the minimum of four, and I encouraged them to do that, since I tried to explain to them that they'd be preserving the history of their own families before it was too late. Then they had to type up the interviews, word-for-word from the tapes."

"Too late?"

"Yeah, like, in my own family, my uncle Fred was the family historian, kinda, but he died and it was then that I'd wished I'd known more about my grandparents and great-grandparents. Too late to find out now…'too late' meaning the people with the stories and information would be gone, too. That's what I mean."

He nodded.

"Okay, they also hadda make a genealogy, you know, a family tree, include memorabilia like photos and certificates and so on…in short, everything they could find, again, before stuff got thrown away when relatives died."

"Anything you read last year stick in your mind?" he asked.

"Yeah, actually, one does, now that I've been thinking about it because of this," I told him.

He leaned forward, suddenly very attentive.

"Go on."

"Well, I read this one kid's project an' he'd interviewed his grandmother on his mother's side, I think it was. In the transcript of the taped interview, she'd said something about something 'terrible' or 'horrible' that his father and uncle had done when they were in high school. I'd asked the kid about it afterwards and he told me he didn't know, an' when he'd asked his granny a follow-up question to it, she'd refused to say anymore an' had just gone on about other things."

"I need the name of the boy," Blake said with a look that told me I couldn't refuse.

"The kid's name is Luther Henshaw."

"Henshaw? You don't happen to know the father's name, do you?!" he asked, now very interested.

I thought for a moment but then shook my head.

"No, the boy was in my non-college class an' not the kind of kid whose parents ever come in for Parents' Night or Open House."

"So Luther would be a senior this year, right?" he asked.

"Yeah."

Blake stood up. "Okay, thanks. This may lead to absolutely

nothing; Henshaw's a common family name around here, probably all over the state...but if his daddy is maybe who I'm thinking of...well, then, maybe. Okay, I'll be talkin' to you, Mr. Finn," he said as he got up, shook my hand, and left. Sticking his head back through the doorway, he added, "By the way, thanks for your help. You have a helluva memory; some witnesses we question can't even remember what they ate the night before for dinner. Thanks again."

And then he was gone.

By that Saturday, I knew I had to find something to do with my hands and mind to take the mind away from the mystery shooter. I knew that if either of us had too much time to think, the worry might start to eat us up. So I decided to give Sandi another cooking lesson, this time in marinara sauce.

"Okay, take the paper husks off those five garlic cloves an' then slice 'em up with this straight razor," I told her, smashing the cloves by giving the flat of the blade a sharp smack with the heel of my hand, handing her an antique razor that I'd found, amazingly without rust, at Max's junk store. "Slice the cloves crosswise as thin as you can."

"Why don't you just use a knife? You have some good sharp ones in the drawer," she asked as she started down at the razor.

"'Cause the razor has a much thinner blade an' it'll let you slice it that much thinner. Just do what I say."

"Yes, *sir*! Remember, I have this razor in my hand!" she growled a little with a twinkle in her blue eyes.

"Oh, gee, I'm scared. You wouldn't dare. Who would you find to give you multiple orgasms?"

She hit me.

"Shut up, you're embarrassing me!"

"What? I can't talk about us?" I asked.

"I love it when you talk about us...just not about what we do in bed."

"That makes no sense. Okay, how about I'll give references to sex code names in case a robin is sitting on the windowsill an' then you won't be embarrassed. I'll call orgasms 'whoopies' an'—*ouch, damn it!*"

I shut up.

While she sliced, I peeled and chopped a small white onion and opened two twenty-eight-ounce cans of Italian plum tomatoes, dumping them, juice and all, into a large stainless-steel bowl.

"Never put tomatoes—or tomato anything—in an aluminum bowl," I told her as I was doing the dumping.

"Why not?" she asked, concentrating on slicing the garlic without slicing her slender fingers.

"Well, the acid in the 'maters'll turn the aluminum black—"

"Yuck!"

"—an' the tomatoes can pick up a metallic taste if they're sitting in the bowl for more than a couple minutes. Hence this stainless bowl. Okay, now watch what I'm doin'."

She paused with her garlic slicing.

"Ya take your hands an' crush the tomatoes until they're all in small, *really* small chunks. If you want a totally smooth sauce, then throw all the tomatoes in the blender. But both of us like the sauce a little chunky, I've noticed…like the sauce on Anthony's pizza."

I squeezed the tomatoes and then put them aside.

Pouring about three tablespoons of extra-virgin olive oil into a large, deep pot, I turned the gas higher under the pot to let the oil heat up.

"The secret to good cooking is never put the veggies into a cold pan an' then turn it on; stuff'll stick. Always use a hot pan, but don't let it get so hot that the olive oil starts to smoke. Olive oil's got a really low flash point. If you're gonna cook with high heat an' oil, use peanut or corn oil, like when I did the Szechwan pork stir fry last weekend."

She nodded.

"Good student!"

She stuck out her tongue and made dog panting sounds.

"Okay, in go the onions. You sauté them until they get translucent and golden, then toss in the garlic for no more than two minutes, an' keep stirrin' so the garlic doesn't burn. Burn the garlic an' it changes from sweet to bitter."

She nodded some more.

"How long for the onions?" she asked.

"About five minutes."

"Then you have time to sit down on that chair so I can sit in your lap so you can lavish me with some weekend kisses," she said, grabbing my wrist and dragging me to the table. I noticed the tape over the bullet holes and reminded myself to remind Pop that he'd promised to replace the pane while we were at work. Then I kissed her, not for as long as she wanted, but I couldn't let the onions burn, either, and I knew from past experience that if we got going too intensely, we could kiss the onions goodbye.

I had her add her garlic and cook it until both the onions and garlic were done. Then I dumped the whole mix, juice included, into the pot, added a tablespoon of the fresh basil we'd kept in the freezer from the summer harvests, and a teaspoon of oregano.

"Now the secret to Mom's marinara," I said, going into the fridge for the jar of currant jelly and a metal tube that looked like a toothpaste tube.

"What's that?" she asked.

"Currant jelly…three tablespoons of this…you can use grape jelly if you can't find currant….and two teaspoons of this," I said, squeezing a long string of something green into a measuring spoon.

"Ugh! What's that?" she asked, staring at the gunk as it snaked in circular rings into the spoon.

"Anchovy paste."

"Yuck! I hate anchovies! Stop!"

"You'll never taste the anchovies, but it's the secret to the flavor. Stop!" I yelled as she tried to take it out of my hand.

I dipped the paste-filled spoon into the mix and it was gone. By that time, the pot had begun to bubble and pop. I brought the whole mixture to a boil, stirred it, and then turned it down to simmer.

"An hour or two, until all the loose liquid is gone…we're gonna add half a cup of red wine in a half hour."

"Umm…yummm! We havin' this for dinner tonight?" she asked, hugging me from behind.

"No."

"*No*?!"

"It's always better the second day; tonight I'm makin' ground-sirloin steaks on the grill."

"Double yum!"

As long as she was happy, it was good enough for me. And it had helped us to forget the two holes in the kitchen window.

That Monday at lunch, Wild Bill would have an idea for The Bunch that would also help us keep our minds occupied, at least for a little while.

26

"Okay, listen, we've all been enjoying the wonderful addition to the administration this year, right?" he asked, looking up from his sandwich.

"What *is* that smell?!" Irene muttered, looking around at the table.

"What?" Bill asked with a guilty look.

"Is that your *sandwich*?!" Deb asked.

"Maybe," he said with a little facial grimace, "it's just fish," he answered defensively.

"How rotten was it when you decided to make a sandwich out of it?" Ray asked.

"Hey, it's just a bluegill I caught," Bill told him.

"When, last Easter?!" I asked, getting my first whiff of something definitely fishy *and* definitely terrible. "That smells like the joke I heard about the blind man and the fish market!"

"What joke?" Sandi asked.

They had all known the joke I meant but they sat there with silly smiles.

"Go ahead, Tom, tell 'er," Irene had murmured slyly.

"Anyway," Bill said, taking me off the hook—although my blond goddess was still staring curiously at me—"we all really love ol' A.H.T. so I thought it'd be fun to have a little contest, with a bet, to find out what those three initials stand for."

"Like what?" Ray asked.

"Well, I was figurin' that we could all put five bucks into the kitty an' the first person who finds out what they stand for gets the dough."

As we were considering the idea, Deb said, "I just figured they stood for Anal something."

"Maybe Anal Hat Tree, since he doesn't seem to use his head for anything more useful," I added.

"I think it's Armpit Heat Tester," Irene offered.

"Figures a chemistry major would work something in about heat," Ray laughed. "Personally, I think they're not initials, they're really a word—*aht*—in an ancient language like Sumerian."

"Meaning what?" Bill asked.

"What else? *Asshole!*" Ray told him.

After the brief laughter, as we all tried to gobble down the remnants of our lunches before our twenty-something minutes were up, we'd all agreed to Bill's suggestion, if only to break up the boredom that sometimes sets in at school. Neither Sandi nor I had told any of them about the shooting, and Pop had fixed the glass by the time Ray and Joanne had dropped by for a glass of wine.

"What joke?" she had asked when we were home that night.

"Huh?"

"Don't 'huh' me! An' stop stallin'. It seemed like everyone at lunch knew what joke you were talkin' about but me! So?"

"Just some bad joke about female odors. I wouldn't insult you by tellin' you it, so stop askin'. If someone tells you some time, you can hear it from him…or her. Not from me. Blame it on the respect I have for you, okay?

"Okay," she said, but she seemed disappointed. I let her stay that way. Then I asked her something I'd been wondering about.

"Hey, goddess, was that custodian Jeck there when you were?"

"Yeah," she said with a little laugh. "He's a little quirky, but do you know the whole story?"

"I don't know anything except he's more than a *little* quirky."

"Well, from what we heard back then, he was a really brilliant guy an' was goin' to VMI—"

"The military school?" I asked, interrupting.

"Yeah, like he was already in his junior year when he was only nineteen, but then a bunch of them enlisted to go to Vietnam an' he got wounded. He's got pieces of that metal stuff in his head—well, his brain, I mean—"

"You mean shrapnel?"

"Yeah, I think that's what it's called. Anyway, he's supposed to be some kinda hero or somethin' an' got a bunch of medals and two or three Purple Hearts, but when he got sent home, they were afraid to operate to try to get all that…shrapnel out because of where it was, an' sometimes I guess the stuff moves around an' affects him."

"Where'd you hear all that?" I wanted to know.

"I had Mr. Meyer for American history in my junior year an' one day the kids were sayin' stuff about Jeck and Mr. Meyer—who was in Vietnam, too—well, he kinda jumped on us and told us about it an' what his patriotism cost him. Mr. Meyer said that when he was still at VMI, Jeck had written a thesis about some battle in World War II that the army still uses to teach strategy or somethin'. In other words, he was supposed to be really, like a genius, until he had that happen to him in Vietnam. It made us all shut up."

Hearing that made me wonder less about Jeck's weirdness and more about why bad things happen to good people. I made up my mind that the next time he asked me about angel-food cake, I'd bake him one.

Blake called us later that night.

"Anything new happen?" he asked.

"No," I told him. "Anything happening at your end?"

"Checked with the school. We wanted to interview the Henshaw boy, but he was absent all last week an' today. We called the house but nobody answered. The truant officer is goin' out to the house tomorrow morning to check on him. Up till now, he's only missed six days of school since ninth grade."

"I don't think he was out at all last year when I had him," I told him, trying to remember.

"He wasn't. Last year was his only perfect year. Any other

thoughts occur to you?"

"No"

"Okay, I'll be in touch," he told me, hanging up.

"Tried to get into Hartley's office but the sonofabitch locks it every time he goes out," Wild Bill informed us at lunch as he struggled with the gristle in the sad piece of roasted something that was sandwiched between two slices of multi-grain bread.

"Well, I tried getting the information out of Bailey in the main office, but she said it was confidential," Deb said. "I told her that I just wanted to put him in the database for the school website but all I got was Bailey's recording of 'I'm sorry but I'm not authorized to blah-blah-blah…'"

"I'm gonna try Betty Handley over in Central Office. She owes me a couple favors from when I had her kid," Bill said.

"That's cheating," Irene said.

"How's it cheating? We don't have any rules!" Bill argued.

"He's right," I told her. "Just whoever finds out first, that's all we agreed on."

"Yeah, yeah, fine," Irene said, wrapping up the rest of her half-eaten store veggie burrito and tossing it deftly into the garbage.

"You been tryin', Tom?" Ray asked me.

I shook my head. "Too busy," I told him.

"Umm…what about you, Sandi?" he asked her.

"Uh-uh, I've got plenty with tryin' to motivate those brain-dead kids in my junior classes. There's a handful in each class who could really get to college, maybe havin' to go to community college first, but they just wanna either get married, go into the military, or go work where their daddies and other male relatives do!"

Most of us nodded; we knew what she was talkin' about.

"Well, if you two lovebirds sit on your asses an' don't try to find out what Hard-On's initials stand for, you might as well kiss your combined ten bucks goodbye," Bill warned.

We just nodded and shrugged. I didn't want to tell him that I was halfway to finding out the answer. Bill's not the most organized guy in the world, and although I was sure he was going to contact that woman in the Central Office, I knew it would take him a while to remember to do it.

    Meanwhile, I had my spies out and mobilized. Joe and Joel were busy.

27

When I left school that day, there was a piece of paper tucked under Baby's wiper. On a piece of lined filler paper, the kind you put in three-ring binders, was a pencil drawing of a tombstone with "*DEad YankEE*" under the letters "*RIP*" printed on it. Yeah, it shook me up but I still thought that it would have been nice if he could have used the right size letters to send an English teacher a death notice. I stuck it in my pocket moments before I heard her coming up from behind me.

"Hi, Sweet Man," she said, giving me a quick peck on the cheek.

We'd started coming in together, once I'd convinced her to get up as early as I had been; with gas prices continually rising, it seemed stupid to have two cars coming to the same place every day from the same place every day. I'm a lot better at getting work done in the morning when the school is empty of both teachers who like to drop by to chat, and students. By the end of the day, even as young as I still am, my ass is usually dragging. Sandi and I'd talked about trying to conserve energy to keep us from falling asleep at nine some tired nights.

"Well, I could have 'em do more work at their desks, or show movies like the social-studies boys, but then I wouldn't be the kind of teacher I wanna be," I told her.

"Yeah, between what Ronnie an' her friends said last year, an' kids I have this year, I hear you put on a real show every day. Where do you find the energy?" she asked.

"I recharge by plugging myself into a beautiful—*oww*! Okay, okay...I don't know; I think I get energized just by the act of teaching. The more I see them smiling or lookin' enthusiastic—which isn't every class, that's for sure—the more I plug into that energy and go with the flow, kinda," I told her. "I'm more tired on the days when we have some kind of testing an' I don't get to teach at all!"

"You musta had some really good role models to be this good this early in your career! Most of my teachers sucked! The only one I really liked and looked forward to going to was Mrs. J. for biology, but she went back to Pennsylvania the year after I had her."

I told her about my eighth-grade social-studies teacher and my senior English teacher and a couple others.

"I guess I'm trying to do some of the stuff an' use the same methods as they did…the two things they all had in common were their enthusiasm about what they taught and their desire to get us kids involved. I could never picture them just lettin' us sit there. I remember how Mr. Meyer used to fidget when we were takin' tests an' he'd be hoping we'd finish before the end of class so he could do something with us. Yeah, good role models…you're right."

Anyway, I didn't tell her about the note on Baby.

When we got home, Sandi trotted down to see Becky about something, so I used the opportunity to call Blake. He wasn't there so I left a message on his answering machine about the note, but told him I didn't want him to call the house because I didn't want Sandi any more nervous than she already was. I figured he'd understand; he did. The next day, he walked into my room during my planning period again, making me glad, for the only time, that Sandi and I didn't have the same one.

"Sorry to take up your school time again. Thought you needed to get brought up to date. First of all, let's see the note."

I gave it to him. He looked at it, looked up at me, then put it in the same thin leather case. Then he said, "Truant officer went out to the house this morning. There were three vehicles in the yard—not counting the seven ones that will never run again—but no one answered the door. Mr. Acton went around the back an' heard a TV on but he couldn't see through the curtains. He went down the road about quarter-mile an' pulled off. About twenty minutes later, Harlan Henshaw came down the road in the pickup that'd been parked in front of their shack. Acton went back to the house and knocked on that back window; the Luther kid peeked out. Acton identified himself an' the kid told him through the window that he was locked in an' the window was nailed shut from outside. An' it was. I'm goin' back there at five with three deputies on suspicion of child abuse. We'll see how that works out. You got a few more minutes?"

"Uhh, yeah, I guess."

"Wanna fill you in on Harlan Henshaw in case he just happens to 'bump' into you sometime. You probably don't know it, 'cause it doesn't get talked about a lot in the county, but we still have some lingering remnants of the pre-integration period in the county...an' there's a semi-active group behind the scenes who are keepin' the Klan alive and well in Page."

"Are you shittin' me—the KKK *here*?!" I gasped, I think.

"That surprise you?" he asked, his eyebrows raised slightly.

"Well, yeah, I guess. I figured this far north, even in Virginia...well, I think of the Klan being still around maybe in Alabama and Mississippi—"

"Prejudice and old ways don't know geography, Mr. Finn...Page County had a helluva time intergratin'. We were at least two years behind most of Virginia. Lots o' bigots, lots o' history—most of it bad...an' the Henshaws and some other in-bred families who think they're rabbits instead of humans...well, they pulled their kids outta the schools when integration came...an' Harlan was one o' them. There's lots o' stories been told about him an' some of his friends an' kin...nothin' anyone could ever prove, but they all had to do with violence. Henshaw family history, guess you could say."

I began to feel a little less cheerful as he continued to talk.

"Anyways, those boys with the white sheets don't do much these days, but we hear they git together now an' then an' talk. We try to keep a quiet eye on them. Guess they don't have much to do, what with them and the ones like them runnin' most of the black folks out. Guess you noticed that there aren't a lot of blacks in the high school."

Funny, I had some black kids in each class but when I actually thought about it, I realized there weren't a whole lot of them in the school...nor did I see many black families in the local stores. I told him that I hadn't noticed.

"Well, for right now, I'd like you to try to start noticin' people who are near you...or maybe behind you...walkin' or in vehicles...an' try to notice it if you see the same vehicle more than once...as for the people—*white* ones...an' ones that look like your basic trailer trash, which is what the kind I been talkin' about do look like."

"You think I'm at risk?" I asked hesitantly.

"Truthfully? Yes, especially after the note you found on your car. By the way, we don't have any recent photos of Harlan, but he's about five-nine, a good two-twenty, at least—mostly fat gut—long black hair an' full beard, usually wears dirty jeans an' a plaid shirt... somewhere in his forties. See anyone like that who seems overly interested in you, or is in a pickup that seems to be followin' you, you watch yourself an' give us a call right away. Truck plate is PYD 565."

He got up, straightening his uniform and picking up the leather case and his hat.

"Just be extra cautious is all I mean. Try not to lose sleep over it. I'll keep in touch; you do the same," he said with a small but tired smile as he left.

"*Yeah, I'll sleep like the dead*," I heard myself say inside my mind.

A couple minutes later, I fired up the new Dell in my classroom that the school had bought for all of us and typed in "history of Luray" on Google.

That night, right after we'd done the dishes, Wild Bill called me, all excited.

"Hey, I just got off the phone with Ray! You hear about the shooting?!" he asked.

"No," I said, feeling my stomach begin to churn.

"Yeah, man, some deputies got shot at some redneck's house. It was all over the scanner! I think most of the sheriff's department's out there! This'd be a good time to rob the bank!" he said with a laugh.

"How bad?" I asked.

"How bad *what*?" Bill asked.

"How bad were the cops shot?" I wanted to know, hoping one of them wasn't the young Siewert fellow.

"Don' know…all there was on the scanner was shit about getting' more cars out there an' sendin' the rescue squad. That's all I know. Told you there's too many goddam guns in this county!" Bill added.

"Let me know if you find out anything else," I told him, "but don't call later'n ten."

He said okay and hung up. I turned to the Harrisonburg station as Sandi was coming out from her shower, toweling the blond hair dry.

"Who was that?"

"Wild Bill. Some shooting in the county. All he knows is some redneck shot some cops," I told her, waiting to see if anything was going to break into the sit-com that was on. Nothing did; no message drifting along the bottom of the screen, either.

The sight of her standing there, the long blue towel gently swinging back and forth across her still-tanned nakedness did a lot to take my mind off the day's events.

"Are you just gonna stare or what?" she asked with a sly smile.

"Gonna do some 'or what' as soon as I take *my* shower," I said, heading toward the bedroom.

No more calls came from Bill. I didn't like keeping anything from her…but I chose silence to having her feeling the way I was.

I did manage to sleep that night. There's a lot to be said for good gin, good food, and the passion that comes with making love. Between the sedation and the exhaustion, sleep had to be inevitable.

28

When we got to school the next morning, news about the shootout at the Henshaw house—or shack—was all over the scanners…and MVHS. I couldn't walk down any hall without hearing someone saying something about what he'd heard.

When Bill joined the Breakfast Club with a box of donuts from one of the local truck stops, he filled us in.

"Redneck's name is Somebody Henshaw—"

"Harlan Henshaw," I interrupted. Sandi gave me a sharp look of surprise.

"Yeah, anyway, the cops went to the house to check on an abuse report or somethin' like that an' he just started shootin' at them. Got one guy in the shoulder an' one in the leg. They're in the hospital but they're gonna be okay. Then the guy started yellin' that he had his kids in there with him an' if the cops tried to break in, he was gonna put them in front of the door an' if one or both o' them got shot, it'd be the sheriff's fault or somethin' like that."

"Why'd he go nuts like that? Do they know?" Irene asked.

Bill shrugged. "All I got was what was on the scanner. They weren't exactly doin' a news broadcast, Irene. Anyway, they staked out the place all night, an' then early this morning, one of the kids busted out a window an' yelled that the old man had got away and not to shoot them."

Sandi was still staring at me curiously, obviously wondering how I knew Henshaw's first name. I tried to not notice, but when she reached down and squeezed my hand, I kind of had to pay attention.

"What?" I said under my breath.

"How'd you know—"

"I'll tell you later...before first period," I said. She let go of my hand but kept sneaking those looks at me until the breakfast gang broke up as the first bell rang.

"Well?"

"Had a long talk with Blake during my planning yesterday," I told her.

"And you didn't think of tellin' me about it?" she asked, frowning and looking a little angry.

"Didn't want you to worry, that's all. I'll tell you after school."

"No! I'm comin' to your room for lunch today. You can tell me then!" she said, marching off down the hall. Yeah, she was a little peeved at me.

"Tom, I'm really scared, really scared," she said with this really helpless look on her pretty face after I'd told her the rest of it.

I sat next to her and hugged her, hoping no kids would drop by early from lunch to spread the word that Mr. and Mrs. Finn used lunch to steal romantic moments.

"What're we gonna do?" she asked.

I couldn't tell her anything...I didn't *know* anything. Blake and Siewert showed up at the cabin around four-thirty that afternoon. *They* told us what we were going to do.

"Mr. Finn, Deputy Siewert here was one of the men who—"

"I remember," I said, shaking Siewert's hand. He had a firm, no-nonsense handshake, not the kind of knuckle-crusher that insecure guys use to try to prove their manhood.

"Folks, you got any place you can maybe go for a few days—relatives, friends, maybe?" Blake asked as he looked back and forth between us as we sat on the sofa; they both stood.

I shook my head.

"All our relatives and friends are right here. Well, we have friends on the faculty, but they all have single-bedroom apartments. Oh, one guy is married and has a house, but he's got three kids an' I wouldn't even think of goin' there," I told them.

"Why do we have to go *anywhere*?!" Sandi said, a little angrily.

"I'm sure you heard about the shooting out at the Henshaw place yesterday (we nodded) an' Harlan Henshaw has a lot of weapons, from what we know. He also has one or two friends an' a whole passel o' kin...an' he's hidin' somewhere around here. We just came from talkin' to his boy Luther, who's as scared of him as you two probably are. He's had that boy locked up for over a week with no food, just water, an' the boy's covered with bruises."

"But why?" Sandi asked.

Blake looked at me strangely, a little curiously.

"You haven't told her?" he asked me.

"Told me what?!" she said, turning to me.

"Just wait, all right?!" I told her impatiently. "Go on," I said, turning back to Blake.

"He evidently was goin' through the boy's room one day an' found that project he did for you an' read it an' went kinda ballistic when he got to Grandma's interview. Luther said he tore out the pages an' made Luther eat them, one by one. Man's kinda mean, wouldn't you say?"

"Sick's more like it," Siewert said, talking for the first time since they'd arrived.

"So what is he afraid of—that I'll find out what that horrible thing he did that the grandmother referred to?" I asked.

"Pretty much points that way, doesn't it?" Blake said with a shrug.

"Tom!" Sandi said, interrupting.

"What?"

"The unit at the resort. We could go there; it'd be only...what, maybe twenty minutes longer to get to school from there?" she asked, looking somewhat relieved.

"The ski place?" Blake asked.

"Yeah. I told you we got a really big wedding present from the

Battaglias...well, that's it," I explained.

"They gave you one of those units up there?!" Blake asked, amazed.

"No, they didn't *give* it to us, but we can use it whenever we want. We haven't even seen it since they opened the place back around Labor Day. Maybe she's right," I said, getting up to get the card and phone number off the refrigerator.

After I'd called up there and cleared our use of the unit—the site manager that reservations had referred me to asked that we not come up until the next day, since the place had never been used and they'd like to get it "aired out and ready for Mr. Battaglia's guests"—Blake had told us that Siewert would be keeping us company that night.

"The deputy will have his car parked behind the office unit. I've already talked to your mother and father an' it's all set."

"You can bunk in here on the sofa if you want," I told him.

Siewert shook his head with a smile.

"Wouldn't do you much good if I was sleepin', would I?" he explained.

"Well, you could just watch TV and nibble if you wanted to," Sandi told him.

"The idea of Deputy Siewert parkin' where he'll be is we're hopin' that maybe Harlan will get desperate an' drop by," Blake explained.

"Oh, great, so we're bait?!" I asked, feeling the heat rise on the back of my neck.

He shook his head.

"No, but since you can't get outta here tonight, we still might get lucky. Meanwhile, I have an idea about Grandma Stewardson," he added.

"Stewardson? Who the hell is that?" Sandi asked.

"Harlan's mama was a Stewardson before she married Harlan's father. When he went to prison, she went back to her maiden name. She's never wanted anything to do with that side of the family since then. Anyway, got an idea. I'll be in touch," he said in his usual parting comment.

Well, Harlan Henshaw didn't pay us a visit that night. I found Siewert awake and looking as if he'd slept eight hours, although I knew he hadn't. He thanked me for the cup of coffee I'd carried down the hill to him. I told him he could leave the cup with Becky.

"Think we might have somethin' goin' for ya today," he said.

"What?"

"Can't really tell you, but just keep your fingers crossed...if you cross your fingers, that is. Have a nice day with the monsters," he added with a chuckle.

"My kids aren't monsters," I told him. "I have this orange plastic bat in my classroom. The first sign of a monster appearing an' out it comes. One good whap over the head with the bat and the monsters disappear," I told him.

He frowned, obviously trying to picture an English teacher with an orange bat.

"Does it work?"

"Oh, yeah."

"Maybe we could adapt it for police work," he said with another smile.

"I think you guys better stick to your regular deterrents; that bat wouldn't stop bullets or knock anyone out."

He just nodded and took another sip.

"Good coffee...thanks."

"Want another cup?" I asked him.

"Nope. I'll be off my shift as soon as you two leave. See you under better circumstances next time, I hope. Have a nice day."

I left.

As we drove down the gravel drive, we waved; he waved back, and as we reached the bottom of the hill and 211, I saw his headlights coming down behind us.

29

I was just unlocking my room when I heard footsteps behind me. The hairs on the back of my neck—and probably every hair on my body—stood up as I felt myself tense as I turned around quickly, feeling my free hand clench itself into a fist. It was only Joe and Joel; Joe was wearing his usual maniacal grin…or leer…and Joel was wearing his usual hair-bush, pointing in all directions.

"Hey, Boss, we got the goods!" Joel whispered secretly, although there was no other person in sight.

"You best have some real good sandwiches for us all next week," Joe told me, reminding me of the deal I'd made with them when I'd sent them off on their spy mission.

"I will. C'mon in," I told them as I held the door and then closed it behind us.

"Here you are," Joe said, handing me a piece of paper. It was a folded envelope addressed to Hartley.

"Where'd you get this?" I asked them.

"Took it outta his mailbox," Joel giggled goofily.

"That's a Federal crime!" I gasped.

"We di'n't open it or nothin'!" Joe said.

"Yeah, we kin put it back!" Joel added.

Slowly, with great trepidation, I unfolded the envelope. It was a junk mail from one of those outdoor-awning-and-enclosed-room-addition companies.

"*Adolph Hilbert Tannenbaum Hartley*" was the first line of the address.

"*Adolph Hilbert Tannenbaum Hartley?!*" I said out loud.

"Yeah, ain' that a dumbass name, Mr. F.?" Joel chortled.
"Yeah, what the hell's a tannenbum?" Joe wanted to know.
"I think it's a family name, Joe, it's not a *thing*," I explained.
"Well, it's still a dumbass name!" he said, scratching his head under his railroad engineer's cap.
"So's Hilbert!" said Joel.
"Okay, you guys, stay here. I've gotta make a copy of this an' then you're gonna take it back an'—wait a minute, how'd you get this?!"
"Aah, we just followed him home a couple days ago an' then we went there yesterday an' got this," Joe explained.
"You didn't skip school, did you!?" I asked with concern.
"Naah, just last period, an' that's Mr. Goodman's class. He'd never miss us," Joel told me.
"How do you know?" I asked, not even remembering who Goodman was.
"He's blind, Mr. F., he can't see a thing!" Joe explained.
"What do you mean, he's blind?! He can't be blind!" I said.
"No, really, the guy's legally blind; he even has a handicapped license plate. Don't you know who he is?" Joel asked.
"I don't think so. What does he teach?"
"He don't teach nothin'," Joel told me. "He's supposed to be teaching business—ya know, business math an' stuff like that. He's the guy who took Miss Perkins' place, remember?"

I guess I'd never heard his name or when the new teachers had been introduced during our week back at the beginning of the school year.

"Anyway," I told them, "you take this back today…but I don't want you to be seen, so make sure—"

"Yeah, yeah, don' worry, we're not nuts," Joel assured me. I assured myself that they were indeed nuts, but I couldn't keep from loving them.

I photocopied the envelope and took the original back upstairs to give to the two weird brothers. I looked forward to seeing The Lunch Bunch. I desperately wanted to tell the news at the Breakfast Club, but there were kids there, too, so I knew it would have to wait until we were in Ray's room for lunch.

"Hey, does anyone know that Mr. Goodman who has Ida Mae's old job?" I asked a few minutes later.

"Yeah, what about him?" one of the senior girls, Sarah, asked.

"I've been told that he's blind," I told her.

"He is!" Ricky, another senior, assured me. "He's got those Coke bottle glasses an' his eyes look like they're three times their size when you look at him!"

"The kids tell me he calls roll an' the kids say 'here' and then sneak out. Sometimes he's there talkin' an' there's only a couple kids left!" Deb said with a laugh. "I didn't believe 'em so I went past his classroom last week—or maybe the week before—and there he was, sitting at his desk, his nose about an inch from the book, reading something about stocks and bonds to the class. I looked in really quick an' there were three girls an' a couple guys in there, and that was all! The girls were just sitting there, talkin' and the two guys were asleep."

"I don't think he'll be here for long if an administrator sees what you saw," Ray suggested.

"Well, I know the kids who have him aren't gonna say anything 'cause everybody gets A's an' they don't want a new teacher who's gonna make 'em do work," Ricky advised us.

I just shook my head, I think, wondering how a legally blind man could even be hired...or get through college...or be able to drive.

"*Adolph Hilbert Tannenbaum?!*" Wild Bill gasped as he began to choke on some of the venison barbecue he'd been dragging from between two halves of a burger roll.

"Are you shittin' me?!" Ray said with a laugh. "What a dumbass collection of names!"

"Jeez, I can't wait for this to get all over the school!" Deb snickered.

"Alas, where is old Ida Mae when we need her?" Irene said with a theatrical sigh. "If she were still here, it'd be news in the first ten minutes!"

"Okay, Tom, how'd you find out? Let's see some proof!" Bill said.

"What—you don't trust me?!" I asked with a hopefully shocked expression on my face.

"Yeah, but let's see the proof anyway," Irene told me.

I pulled out the sheet of paper with the copy of the envelope.

Bill snatched it out of my hand and stared at it, then passed it to Deb. As it made its way back to Sandi, who was sitting in her usual place to my left, Irene asked, "Where'd you get it?"

"Can't tell. I had some spies out there an' they came through for us," I told them.

"Came through for *you*, you mean!" Ray reminded me. "You're the one who's gonna get the money."

"Gee, take away the ten bucks Sandi and I put in…golly gee, a whole twenty bucks! Whoo, I can buy a case of Corona Light now!" I said, acting overly excited.

"Hey, you wanna give *me* the twenty bucks? I'll be glad to drink your beer," Wild Bill suggested.

"That's okay. I have to use some of the dough to buy cold cuts to feed my two spies all next week," I informed them.

"Huh?" Sandi said.

"I told them I'd make them lunch for a week if they found out Hartley's full name. So now I make them lunch."

"Well, sweetie, since you're gonna be doing that, you can make *my* lunch all next week, too," Sandi announced.

"Yes, dear," I said humbly as I caught her winking at Irene and Deb.

"My God, this is gorgeous!" Sandi gasped when I opened the door to #17 at the Blue Ridge Resort. I'd been in resort condos and motels before, but this was really lavish. As we entered, we could see a large living room directly in front of us. A few steps in and a pretty good-sized kitchen with a bar-like island separated itself from a dining area with a full-sized table and six chairs. That opened up on the right side to the same living area. We'd find the two bedrooms, both with king-size beds to the far left, and a huge bathroom with a two-sink counter that stretched along one whole wall; a huge Jacuzzi and a stall shower finished it off. A faint hint of lilacs came from somewhere.

On a table in the living room, in front of a large-screen television, were three bottles: two bottles of local Virginia wine, one Cabernet, the other a Reisling; the third bottle was Dom Perignon.

"Holy shit!" I said, "Dom Perignon! You ever had expensive champagne like this?!" I asked her.

"That André stuff a couple times…and whatever that better stuff was that Pop bought for Christmas last year when you gave me the ring," she said. "Not like this."

"Wonder if it's really that much better…Jesus, I think a bottle o' this stuff is close to a hundred bucks…maybe more."

When I opened the refrigerator to put the champagne in, I was jolted by what I saw. Inside, a slight haze of chill on them, were a good dozen bottles of Corona Light and another dozen of Rolling Rock. On the door was a green bottle of Tanqueray gin. I was very, very happy that Gerry Battaglia had decided to like me. I began to wonder how he'd found out…and then I decided that I didn't want to know. We had enough trouble with Harlan Henshaw.

The small card in a blue resort envelope that had been propped up against the champagne read:

Enjoy. Use everything. G.B.

We'd never made love in a Jacuzzi before; we used every inch of it that night. We saved the champagne for something special.

30

Becky and Pop had both been upset about the need for us to go into what could only be called "hiding." Pop was still steaming about the whole shooting incident and had not stopped muttering about arming himself and waiting in ambush. Once the three of us had gotten him calmed down, Becky had still been upset about our leaving.

"Mom, it'll only be for a little while," Sandi had assured her over the phone from the resort the next afternoon.

"Yeah, tell her that the deputy told me yesterday morning that they might break something soon," I called from the kitchen where I was chopping up some onions for a homemade pizza.

"Mom, Tom said….oh, okay—*she heard you!*" she called to me. "Yeah…no, I don't think so…okay…okay…no, *don't* tell Ronnie! She'll freak!" Sandi semi-shouted into the phone. "Okay…yeah, okay…yeah, okay, every day. Give Pop our love. Okay," she said and hung up.

"You gonna do the dough this time?" I asked her, having taught her how to spread pizza dough out on the pan.

"Is it ready?"

"No, about half an hour. Gotta let it get warmer."

"Can you make us a couple martinis?" she asked. "I need something to put me out tonight. This waitin' is killing me…and you. Stop tryin' to be so strong for both of us. I can handle it."

"You just said it's killin' you…that's not 'handling it'!" I told her.

"Whatever. Do we have onions?"

"What, for the gin?"

"Yeah."

"No, I didn't think of anything like that when we packed for our unexpected getaway. Think you can live without them?" I asked.

"Well, since you've gotten me used to them...and now likin' them...let's pick some up on the way home tomorrow afternoon, okay?"

"Sure. We're gonna need to put a little shopping list together. Gerry didn't stock the cabinets with food, just the liquid kind."

"You think we're gonna be here that long?" she asked with a genuine look of concern.

"Hope not. We'll just buy enough to get through the weekend, okay? Anything we don't use we can take home. It's not like we're on vacation hundreds o' miles away from the cabin," I assured her.

"What would we have done if we hadn't had this place to escape to?" she asked with a sigh.

"We'd be stickin' it out back home, I guess," I said with a shrug. "Either that or we'd have gone to another motel...an' that could've gotten expensive fast, 'cause we would've had to eat out all the time. Motels rooms don't have kitchens."

"Well, we could've....no, I guess we couldn't," she started to say.

"What?" I asked.

"I was gonna say we coulda eaten with Mom and Pop, but that woulda put us—and them—in harm's way. Oh, shit, I just hope they get that bastard soon!" she snapped angrily.

As if it were part of a script, that was when the phone rang.

"Hello?" I said hesitantly.

"Blake here. You two settled in all right?" he asked.

"Yeah, we're both settled an' *unsettled*!" I told him.

"Well, if you could stand a little company, I have some good news for you."

"Uhh...yeah, I guess, if it's important. I mean, we were plannin' an early bedtime tonight, Blake. We're both pretty worn out…teachin's tirin' enough without this stuff."

There was a very brief silence.

"Aah, I guess I just wanted to tell you in person. Okay, here's the latest: we got Grandma's minister, Reverend Payne, to go talk to her about what she'd said on the interview tape—which Luther still had, by the way. It took Reverend Payne a while he said; she seemed torn between her faith and her family, but he finally convinced her of what the Lord would want her to do and he brought her in to talk to us early this afternoon. We have the whole thing on tape."

"And…?"

"Okay, I'll give you the condensed version: she told us that Harlan, his half-brother Whittaker, and two other boys were the ones responsible for an unsolved murder and arson that goes all the way back to 1970. I'll give you the long version some other time, but the short version is that back then, a black minister was trying to have an old building in Luray that used to house slaves who were going to be auctioned off torn down, but it was on Federal property an' the locals in charge couldn't—and probably wouldn't—do anything about it. Well, one night, the whole place burned to the ground with that minister in it. When the fire was out, they found what was left of the man inside, tied to a brick upright with barbed wire. They later found out that he'd also been shot multiple times and he'd been somewhat…umm…mutilated. Anyway, looks like we've finally learned who did that; now all we have to do is find them. Guess that's what the 'horrible thing' that Grandma referred to was. Poor old lady—she's in her seventies—was pretty shook up by the time we'd asked all the questions we needed to. She just kept sayin' she hoped Jesus would forgive her…and her son."

"Jesus!" I muttered.

"Yeah. Nice fellas, I know," Blake said. "We've got APB's out on all three of them," he told me.

"I thought you said there were four."

"One got killed in Vietnam the following year. The rest are still around here. They don't know that we've talked to Granny, or what she's told us, so we should be able to grab the other two right quick.

I'll get back to you. Hang in there," he said and hung up.
I told her what Blake had told me. I think a slight sense of relief descended on us, but I could tell that we wouldn't really feel better until they had Henshaw and the others behind very secure bars. I think the pizza *did* taste a little better that night than it might have if we hadn't gotten Blake's phone call.

The Lunch Bunch handed over the twenty bucks the next morning and during my planning period, I found Joe and Joel, both in their fourth year of auto shop, to tell them to stop by the Breakfast Club each morning the following week to pick up their lunches.

"Don't give me no egg salad or tuna or bologna!" Joel said.

Joe hit him on the side of the head with a ratchet wrench with a spark-plug socket on it.

"*Oww, you fu*—! Damn it, that hurts!" Joel muttered.

"Don't be disrespectful to Mr. F. He's the boss. If he wants to give ya dogshit on a bun, you'll take it!" Joe growled.

"Okay, okay, no egg salad, bologna, or tuna. Anything *you* don't like, Joe?" I asked.

"Well, sir, since you asked, I would prefer not getting any egg salad, tuna, bologna, *or* liverwurst. Liverwurst always kinda reminded me of Alpo...if that is acceptable, sir," he explained very politely...and out of character.

"I would be very happy to provide you with delicious lunches made of the finest victuals," I responded in kind to both of them, giving them each a slight bow.

"Cool!" said Joel, still rubbing the side of his head.

"We'll be there, Mr. F.," Joe assured me. I was sure they would be. I filled their week with a new kind of sandwich every day, from meatballs to roast beef to grilled chicken and so on. They would beg me to make their lunches every day after that.

"C'mon, Mr. Finn, we'll pay ya ten bucks a day to do it!" Joel pleaded.

"Where you gonna get ten bucks a day?!" Joe asked him sarcastically.

"I'll steal it from my old man if I hafta. He falls asleep drunk every night. He'd never miss it!"

I just shook my head.

"Fellas, I'd love to, but one, I don't have the time in the morning, really, and two, I wouldn't take your money...or your father's," I said, giving Joel The Look. "Sorry."

They looked predictably disappointed, but then Joe's expression brightened and he said, "Well, if you need some more jobs done, then will ya ask us and then we could do the same deal? How about that?"

"Okay, if I need henchmen again for another tricky job, you'll be the first ones I'll call, okay?" I told them.

They walked away happy, I think.

31

The police arrested the two other suspects, Henshaw's half-brother and someone named Shelton Lewis, at their homes without incident; both had been asleep at four in the morning. Then they got the big break in regards to Henshaw.

Evidently, Harlan's alcoholic needs had overruled his sense of safety...or he had simply believed that he could come out of the woods he'd been hiding in, go to one of the out-of-the-way Mom-and-Pop groceries, get his supplies, and get back safely. Maybe he'd been right; unfortunately, two deputies had been coming down the same road he was going the other way on. They'd recognized the truck.

"Didn't even hafta look at the license, they knew it was Harlan's pickup," Blake told us that evening at the resort. "Dumb shit had two revolvers, a deer rifle, an' a shotgun with him where he was hidin' in an old hunter's shack on the mountain between Luray and Edinburg...an' he left 'em all up there. The whole thing coulda been nasty if he'd been armed, but he wasn't. We got a sample of his saliva from a cup he was drinkin' from when he was bein' interrogated. Already sent that to a lab along with the Marlboro butts we found out back behind you. We'll know in a couple days if we got a DNA match. We'll be doin' a ballistics on the deer rifle, too; got a feeling we'll get a match there, too. That'll just be part of his problems. With the taped testimony of his mama and her sworn statement, he's already facing Federal charges for arson and murder, as well as violation of the dead minister's civil rights...an' shootin' at you if the rifle matches. I wouldn't lay too much money on Harlan

Henshaw or his two buddies seein' freedom again. I'm sure they'll wanna try him in Federal court since the building he burned down and the man he killed were on Federal property, but Virginia prosecutors might wanna have something to do with it all, too; we got the death penalty in this state, you know. Might put a big piece of bad history to bed once an' for all."

"What about his pals in the white sheets?" I asked.

"I think this'll put what's in their bowels in their pants when this all comes out. There ain't all that many of them to begin with, an' I'd bet a month's salary that we prob'ly got the top three…or at least, the ones apt to do more than just talk about doin' bad things," he explained.

"Whew, that's a relief!" I said, looking at Sandi sitting next to me; she nodded.

"Interest you in a beer?" I offered Blake before I'd thought about it. He smiled and shook his head.

"Sorry, not a good thing to do on duty…but I *will* take you up on that some hot summer day when I'm drivin' past the Alpine…an' I'm *not* on duty. How's that?" as he stood up and offered me his hand.

"Deal. An' don't you forget. You helped us a lot with our nerves," Sandi said, taking his hand as well.

"And I know, you'll be in touch," I said as he began to open his mouth. He stopped, smiled, shook his head, and pulled the door closed behind him.

"Gives you a different picture of the Southern cop," I said.

"They're not all like him," Sandi warned me, "depends on the county. But they're not all like the ones on *Dukes of Hazzard*, either."

"We coulda been in deep shit if he was like Barney Fife!" I told her. Sandi let out the first good laugh I'd heard from her in weeks…and she just kept going until she ran out of breath. It was nice to be back…and nicer to make her laugh again. Just making her meals would never be enough.

We had the bottle of Dom Perignon that Saturday night, back at the cabin…although we both agreed that we wished we could've taken that Jacuzzi back home with us.

A couple weeks later, on a Wednesday afternoon, Sandi and I headed down to Harrisonburg to pick Ronnie up for her first fall break, all of five days. The blond imp had managed to catch a ride up from Blacksburg with a suitemate who'd been willing to drive Ronnie all the way home, but we had told Ronnie we'd pick her up in Harrisonburg and treat us all to lunch.

"Cool! The leaves are just changin' up here! They're almost gone down in Blacksburg!" she'd chirped when we were driving back through Stanley. "What's new?"

All through lunch she'd chattered on and on about college—her classes, the new friends she'd made, her suitemates, and the new surroundings. She'd put on a few pounds, but she'd needed to, and I'd already warned her about "the freshman fifteen," which Sandi had never heard of since she'd commuted back and forth to college for the four years.

"You look good, Ronnie," I'd told her. "Turnin' into a real heartbreaker."

She'd beamed and then, with a frown, had asked, "You mean I ain't 'Slim' anymore?"

"Naah, you're still slim, but you don't look like a stick anymore…an' I think there's still a chance you might even grow a nice butt," I said, wanting to remind her that I was never going to stop ribbing her.

"Mark says I have a nice one right now!" she'd snapped, sticking her tongue out at me.

"Have you two been keepin' in touch?" I'd asked, knowing full well that they'd been keeping up an Internet romance as best as they could. Every time Sandi and Becky had talked to Ronnie on the phone, the conversation had always gone to the two lovebirds.

"Of course! Doesn't your wife tell you anything?!" Ronnie had asked.

"Oh, yeah, guess it just slipped my mind, what with everything else that's been going on." Then we told her.

"He shot holes through the window at you?! *Oh my God*! Weren't you scared?! Holy shit! Why didn't anybody tell me about all this stuff?!" she jabbered non-stop.

We got her calmed down enough to stop bouncing all over the backseat of Baby; Sandi told her everything we knew up to that time, which was that they were moving the trial to Winchester, and that the three murderers would be tried by Virginia prosecutors.

"When's the trial?" she asked.

"Sometime before Christmas but after Thanksgiving. They wanna get it over with before the holidays, though, so the jury doesn't hafta have their Christmas ruined. Last thing I heard on the news was December second, I think," I told her.

When we pulled up to the Alpine office, there was an unfamiliar car parked to the right, a rental Lexus.

"Anyone you know?" I asked Sandi.

"Nope. Probably a tourist…they're all over the place 'cause of the fall foliage, remember?"

"Oh, yeah."

It wasn't a tourist; when we walked in with Ronnie, I saw Becky standing behind the counter with a very mischievous look on her face.

"Who's—"

"Boo!" came from behind us, making all three of us jump and Sandi let out a little yelp.

As the door swung closed, there stood Mark Battaglia and his father, both with rather dumb smiles on their faces.

"Aaahh…guhhh….oh my *God*! Aaaahh!" Ronnie screamed as she jumped up and wrapped her thin legs around Mark. Gerry Battaglia stood aside to avoid being knocked into the wall.

I heard laughter coming from behind us; it was Pop and Becky. Pop had been down behind the counter, for some reason. I guess it was supposed to be part of the surprise conspiracy.

"OhmyGodOhmyGodOhmyGod*OhmyGod*!!" Ronnie just kept

saying until Mark unhooked her arms and legs and more or less lowered her to the floor...although it looked as though she were still somewhat levitated by the unexpected surprise.

"Where'd you come from?! How'd you get here?!" she said, almost out of breath.

"Dad's got a buddy who flies. We flew into Luray's little airport an hour ago. Your mom knew all about it," he explained.

Sandi and I both looked at Becky, who just shrugged and held her arms out, palms up in the standard sign of "hey, what could I do?"

"Mark wanted it to be a big secret, so I decided that the fewer people who knew, the better, is all," she explained.

"Are you staying up at the resort?" I asked Gerry Battaglia.

"Well, Jake—that's my pilot pal—and I are. Your mother-in-law thought maybe Mark'd like to stay down here since he's got to go back to Williamsburg on Saturday—"

"Saturday?! Can't ya stay till Sunday?!" Ronnie asked.

"Ronnie, we've gotta drive *you* back to Harrisonburg Sunday morning, remember?" I told her.

"Oh...yeah," she said with a pout. Then she smiled. "We can put him in Sandi's old room, right?!" she asked Becky, brightening up again.

"Already fixed, bed's made...ready for occupancy," Pop told her.

"Wheeee!" Ronnie yelled, putting her arms around Mark all over again and burying her face in his chest.

Gerry just smiled and shook his head. Then he looked at me.

"Heard you had a reason to use the unit. Everything okay?" he asked softly.

"Yeah, it's a beautiful unit...and we've never been that spoiled by anyone before," I assured him.

He nodded matter-of-factly and then shook his head a little.

"Not quite what I meant. Glad you like the unit...but everything all right concerning the reason you had to camp out up there?"

Another one of those jolts went through me. He knew what had been going on, all right. And I said another silent prayer of thanks that Gerry Battaglia had taken a liking to me...and us.

"Yeah, all cleared up," I told him.

"Good. But use the place for more than an emergency, okay? I don't wanna pay the upkeep on a deserted unit...an' winter's almost here. Learn to ski or somethin', huh? Or just go up an' look at snow," he told us, looking back and forth between Sandi and me. "Well, I'll leave the lovebirds in your care. I'll be back to get this poor befuddled fool around nine Saturday morning; that okay?" he'd asked Becky.

"Sure, but you might have to surgically remove my youngest from him," she said with a chuckle. "If you wanna make it a little later, I could treat y'all, including the pilot, to a real Southern breakfast."

Battaglia shook his head with a genuine look of regret.

"I'd love to, but we hafta get Mark back to school so I can get myself back to Jersey...Sunday's gonna be a workday for me. Sorry, but thanks," he said as he gave us a backhand wave and went out to the Lexus.

Needless to say, Ronnie had an unexpectedly wonderful fall break. Sandi had let them use her Mustang, and other than breakfasts and dinners, we'd seen very little of them. After all, it was *their* fall break.

32

In the aftermath of the Henshaw business, the tests had made positive DNA matches between the cup he'd drunk from and three of the Marlboro butts; they'd sent samples of the hair of both the half-brother and the Lewis man and had matched the other two butts to Lewis, who had decided to try to avoid the death penalty by copping a plea and turning state's evidence against the other two. The bullets matched Henshaw's 30.06 rifle as well, adding attempted murder to the other, more serious, charges. The trial had taken a total of two days; no lawyer within a hundred miles had been willing to take the cases of the three murderers, and the public defenders appointed to them had had nothing to use to defend the men with, and then, with the sudden willingness of Lewis, who must have seen the death penalty looming, to testify, that had pretty much made it an easy case for the jury to decide. Indeed, they'd deliberated for only a half-hour before they'd presented the judge with their decision.

Lewis' testimony—what with questioning and evidence from when the horror had taken place back in 1970—had taken up most of one whole day, and had been covered by two Harrisonburg TV stations and three newspapers. The best, or most thorough account, had been in the Harrisonburg daily.

Lewis had testified that the four men—then all between eighteen and twenty-one—had been drinking pretty heavily that day, and then had followed the black minister home after he had led a protest in front of the old structure that had once been a holding area for slaves brought into the Luray area. They had broken in, beaten him, tied him up, and then, when it had gotten dark, had driven back the old building. There, they had wired him to the pillar with barbed wire and had done a number of unmentionable acts of sick brutality to the old man. Then they had poured kerosene all over him and the interior of the building and had set fire to it.

Lewis told the court that they had driven off immediately, but that Harlan Henshaw had stopped at a high point above town so that he—or they—could "enjoy watching a nigger barbecue." The news account described the shocked and outraged expressions on the faces of the jurors—half black and half white—when Lewis had uttered that phrase.

In the sentencing after the guilty verdict the following day, the judge had told all three men that "your acts defy the word *human*, and if we did not live in a humane society, I would find a way to punish you in the same manner that you took the life of that man." As it was, on the recommendation of the jury, he had sentenced Henshaw and his half-brother to death by lethal injection, and the Lewis man to forty years with no opportunity for parole, basically saying that he would die in prison, since all three men were pushing fifty.

"And let the rest of those following this trial, who have not yet come to grips with the concept that we are *all* Americans and *humans* under the Constitution, *regardless of race*, be warned and reminded that there is no statute of limitations on crimes as vile as the one that we have had the disgusting displeasure to have had to listen to in this courtroom!" the judge had added before he had proclaimed the end of the trial and its proceedings.

Christmas seemed to come faster that year, maybe because the vacuum left behind by the closure of our personal crisis had just sucked the days up until we were all, once again, sharing a second Christmas together. Sandi and I had insisted on everyone spending Christmas Eve with us; it was a little crowded, because Ray and Jo had decided not to go north that year in order to save some money for a future house. We'd had an open house all the day, and had been visited by a constant stream of students and friends, both from

Sandi's childhood and college, as well as the Lunch Bunch, with the exception of Irene, who'd gone back to Jersey for the holidays.

By early evening, only the six of us were left in front of the fire crackling in the fireplace; Ronnie had received an early Christmas present: a round-trip ticket to Jersey and back, and I'd driven her down to Charlottesville to catch an early Thursday flight to Newark. You don't have to figure out who the plane tickets were from, or where she'd be staying. I was eager to hear her talk when she returned after experiencing the ethnic traditions of the totally Italian family; she wasn't even close to knowing what she was about to experience...and I suspected that she might come home ten pounds heavier.

The fall and first few days of winter had been without any snow at all, except for one afternoon in late November when one huge gray cloud had passed over MVHS, leaving a few hundred thousand snowflakes, getting the kids all excited, before the cloud had moved on and the sun broke back through the remaining clouds and we could hear a long, sustained groan from the entire student body.

As I sat in front of the fire with her, with Jo in Ray's lap in the large chair and Becky and Pop cuddled together on the small sofa, a Johnny Mathis Christmas CD playing in the stereo I'd bought during the summer, life seemed better than good.

"It don't get much better than this," Pop had said, as if he'd been reading my thoughts.

"Yeah, Pop...but wouldn't you rather be back down in Florida with Aunt Hildy?" Sandi asked him with a wink to me.

"Sure...about as much as I'd like to be getting a root canal right now!" he grunted.

"Y'know, Tom, a lot's happened in our first year-and-a-half," Ray observed.

"Yeah, an' I hope it gets a lot calmer and quieter from now on!" I told him. "No more kidnapings, no more almost-murders, no more psycho English teachers, no more gossiping bitches—"

"Ha! That'll be the day!" Becky said with a laugh.

"Okay, scratch that one..."

"How about a new head librarian who likes *all* the kids and one new assistant principal?" Ray suggested.

"I have a feeling old Hartley might be thinking of applying somewhere else. I think he's pretty much had it with all the kids yelling "Heil Hitler!" when his back is turned," Sandi injected.

"Or 'Hey, Hilbert!'" I added.

"That's someone's name? *Hitler Hilbert?*" Becky gasped.

"No, Mom, it's Adolph Hilbert, but that's bad enough!" Sandi told her.

"Don't forget the Tannenbaum," I reminded her. "His whole name is Adolph Hilbert Tannenbaum Hartley, Becky," I explained.

"Good God!" she exclaimed.

"Hey, look!" Jo had semi-shouted, pointing to the windows on either side of the fieldstone fireplace chimney.

As we looked, large fluffy flakes had begun to drift past the window. I got up to turn on the back spotlight so we could see them out the back.

"Son, gonna install some spots on your front and side so we can really light 'em up next year," he told me.

"Why wait till next year, Pop? You and I'll go down to Lowe's the day after Christmas. There's gonna be more snow between now an' spring." And we did.

We'd agreed to open one present each on Christmas Eve and the rest Christmas morning, down at Becky and Pop's, which is where the bulk of the presents were sitting under their large Frazier fir.

We'd gotten Ray and Joanne a set of T-Fal pots and pans, and Mom and Pop two really good Italian cookbooks and a pasta maker. Sandi and I got a ravioli attachment for our own pasta maker from Ray and Jo, and a KitchenAid mixer, complete with every possible attachment, from Mom and Pop. Everyone was happy, for sure.

Around eleven, Ray and Jo left with large yawns, followed right after that by the parents—one of mine, one of hers—and now, both of both of ours.

And after late showers, Sandi had decided that she would take the lead in deciding whether we were going to sleep right after that or not. We didn't go to sleep right after that.

    There was still Christmas day, of course, and the snow was still drifting down as I went back out into the kitchen to shut off the outside lights. I looked to the left at the new pane of unholed glass, took a deep breath, smiled—I think—and went back to the woman who owned my heart.

33

As we were all recovering from the Christmas meal in Becky and Pop's living room, we got a call from Ronnie; as usual, the dinner had been enough to feed twice as many as the six of us. Sandi put the call on the speakerphone.

"Holy jeez, you wouldn't believe the food, Mom! Oh my God, we started eatin' at three this afternoon an' they're *still* eatin'! I've never seen so much food…and Mom, now I know what T. meant when he told our classes that we didn't know what real Italian cooking an' food was like until we went north. God, I had the best lasagna in the world! An' there must be sixty people here…well, some come for a while an' go…Mark must have a thousand relatives…an' the tree's ten-feet tall an' the house…you could put all of the motel units in it, I bet! Oh my God, there's—*hey!*" We could tell that someone had grabbed the phone from her.

"Hi, it's me, Mark. She's exaggerating (*No, I'm not!*" we could hear in the background), but I think she's havin' a good time an' all my relatives love her accent…although she's havin' a real hard time with ours!" he added with a laugh.

"Mark?" I called out.

"That you, Mr. Finn?"

"Yeah…uhh, how's M.D.?" I asked hesitantly.

There was a pause at his end.

"She's okay…Dad has her in a private school this year—all girls—an' she's dealin' with it. But she's really cleaned up the look…if you know what I mean."

I thought I did.

"Tell her I said hello an' if she needs a letter for college, let me know. I owe you, too."

He laughed.

"You mean you could lie that well?"

"It wouldn't be lies...maybe just some slight exaggerations. Anyway, your dad's...well, your family's been good to us. My way of saying thanks, this time, I guess."

There was a brief, very brief, silence, and then Mark said, "That's really cool of you. I'll tell Dad."

"Okay, but tell M.D., too. Understand?" I said.

"Yes. Yes, sir. See, I did pick up something from bein' down South. Anyway, here's the Blond Terror again. Merry Christmas—that's from me and my parents, by the way. Dad said to make sure I told you that."

"Merry Christmas!" we all shouted back at the speakerphone.

Ronnie chattered on for another ten minutes, telling us that she was going to need an extra suitcase to hold all the presents she'd received.

When we picked her up at the airport four days later, she hadn't brought a second suitcase, but there were two large, heavily taped boxes waiting at the luggage area, along with her one suitcase.

"All those are presents?!" Sandi had exclaimed, her blue eyes wide.

"Well, there's a few surprises in there for Tom...an' you, I guess. You'll just hafta wait an' see."

She did look ten pounds heavier, but it was probably just the bulky ski sweater and the down parka she was wearing. I did notice, too, that her butt was filling out nicely...although I didn't think she'd ever come close to the one my wife took my breath away with...when she wasn't taking my breath away with something else.

When we got home, Ronnie opened the boxes to show us an avalanche of presents—mostly clothes, books, perfumes...and a very beautiful and old, I was sure, cameo brooch—that she'd received. Then she'd made me close my eyes as she put my surprises on the coffee table.

"Okay, you can open your eyes now," she informed me a minute or two later.

On the table was a huge assortment of Italian appetizers and dry sausages: stuffed hot peppers, artichoke hearts, expensive balsamic vinegars and infused olive oils, cappicola and soppresata, smoked provolone, and six loaves of crusty Italian bread.

"Mr. B. got the bread just before we left for the airport," she said.

"He said either freeze it or eat it right away!" she ordered.

"Yes, dear," I said.

Looking at Sandi, I said, "You don't even know what you're looking at, do you?"

She shook her head.

"Well, you will by the time we finish all this," I informed her.

"Damn, what a spread!" Ray, the only true Italian in the room said, practically drooling.

I took a jar of each treat and two of the sausages and tossed them to him.

"Here," I said.

"Hey, I can't take these! You can't find stuff like this in Luray!" he argued.

"Oh, shuddup. It's Christmas, so Merry Christmas."

"Okay, okay, but you can have these back," he said, tossing the sausages back, and reminding me that he was now a vegetarian.

"Oh, jeez, I forgot Skinny there made you convert to eating only grass and dirt," I said with a wink toward Sandi.

"Hey!" Joanne said, "just because—"

"Yeah, yeah, I know, 'just because you don't have twenty pounds of undigested meat in your intestines doesn't give me the right to call you Skinny,' right?"

"Right, Buster!" she said with a laugh.

"And as I told you before, it may not give me the right, but it sure gives me the reason….but thanks. Now I get to eat all this good meat *and* fat all by myself!"

She just shook her head and laughed some more.

Yeah, Merry Christmas in Virginia…again.

34

The day we returned from Christmas break, I got a late present—of inner laughter—from Tammy. Remember Tammy, the hair-sprayed blond cosmetic explosion?

Well, we were all munching on breakfast when she came into the room with a smile of utter ecstasy on her artificial face. She went straight to Deb, whom she had for a computer class.

"Look, Miss R.!" she'd said, holding out her left hand.

Deb kind of squinted at the hand and said, "What?"

"The ring, the ring! See my ring?!" Tammy gushed.

As those of us close enough looked, I could see a thin gold band on her left ring finger; I wasn't absolutely sure, but I thought I could see something tiny twinkling a little, too.

"I'm pre-engaged!" Tammy announced. "Lucas asked me to get engaged at Christmas! Isn't that too cool?!"

"Pre-engaged? What the hell is that?" Wild Bill asked.

"It means that we're gonna get engaged, an' now we're pre-engaged to get engaged, see?" Tammy explained slowly, as though she had to remember how to explain it.

"What a crock o' shaving cream!" Bill laughed. "It's just another sneaky way of getting' more jewelry outta some poor slob!"

"It is *not*!" Tammy said, stamping her foot. I recall having the thought that I hadn't seen anyone stamp a foot in a long time...like maybe fifth grade. "It means that he loves me an' wants to marry me someday an' when he gets more money, he's gonna git me a real engagement ring!" she insisted.

"So this isn't really a real ring then?" Irene asked.

"Huh?"

"You just said that when he gets more money (*'Ah-ha!' said Bill*), he's gonna buy you a *real* ring, so that must mean that this isn't a real ring, right?" Irene explained slowly, in her case because she knew whom she was talking to.

"*NO!* We are *pre-engaged*! Doesn't anybody get it?!" Tammy asked, looking around desperately hopeful, her smile of ecstasy no longer anywhere near her face.

"I get it, Tammy," I told her.

"See?!" she said triumphantly, "Mr. Finn understands, don't you?" she announced, turning back to me.

"Sure. You're pre-engaged, which means you can now have pre-pre-martial sex, an' you can get pre-pregnant if you don't use pre-birth control, but if you don't want the baby, you can get a pre-abortion or put it up for pre-adoption, an' then you can get pre-married, an' if that doesn't work out, you two can get pre-divorced an' you can collect pre-alimony, an'—." That was when she turned and stormed out.

When the laughter had died, Deb wiped her eyes and said, "Don't worry, all her bubble-brained friends in my class will all be suitably impressed an' jealous."

The second half of my second—and Sandi's first—year seemed to fly by. She struggled, trying to motivate the slackers, tolerate the whiners, and encourage those who were really trying. Half of our conversations that year were about teaching, as can be imagined, and, given what had happened that day, whether it was really worth it, especially when we got our paychecks and looked at the difference between the amounts next to "gross pay" and "net pay."

I constantly had to convince her that she needed to focus on the successes and on the kids she was reaching, rather than to take home the one or two hemorrhoids who had made her day difficult.

"But some of them, you just wanna strangle!" she'd said one day on the drive home.

"I've had more parents I'd like to strangle than kids," I told her. "If they'd done better jobs, we wouldn't have to deal with the lack of respect or the total lack of work ethic or pride. I want to tell some of these mothers that they should've duct-taped their knees together if they didn't want to take the pill!"

She'd laughed, a little ruefully.

"Why do we do it?" she said, leaning back with a sigh.

"Because it's the most important job in the world. If we do a shitty job, we risk sending them out into the world to find shitty jobs and shitty lives because we only gave them a shitty chance at success. It reminds me of something I heard John Crowe telling one of his English students outside his room last year."

"What did he say?"

"I was just passing by an' I'm not sure what the kid had just said, prob'ly something like whatever he was doin' was okay with him, an' John got pretty much nose-to-nose with the kid and said something close to: *'If C's are good enough for you, then you will only get a C-job which will only allow you to lead a C-life, only attract a C-girl, have a C-marriage, and when you look back on your life, it'll never have any A's or B's in it…and the worst thing is, your own children will follow the same mediocre pattern forever because all you could give them were C-chances. Is that what you want for yourself?"* something like that."

"Wow! I'm gonna use that some day!" she exclaimed. "That is *so* true! Maybe I oughta observe him. He wasn't here when I was."

"He came here two or three years ago from Ohio, I think. The one thing I've heard John complain about, the few times I've been with him, is the willingness of so many of these kids to settle for mediocrity…like what their parents have is good enough. It's the old hope-I-can-get-a-doublewide-someday attitude," I grumbled. "So, darlin', since you asked, *that's* why we're doin' this!"

"I love you so much!" she sighed, reaching across the console and kissing me on the ear. "Ol' Mr. Passionate, that's my man."

A few weeks later, she had a major moment that told her she needed to be doing what she was doing.

She'd been teaching a piece of adolescent lit called *Lisa, Bright and Dark*, and the kids in that particular class were arguing points about Lisa's parents and what Lisa's friends had done. The book's about a teenage girl who's going crazy—hearing voices, suffering violent mood swings—and her parents don't want to deal with it, choosing instead to insist that she's "just going through a phase" or that she's been watching too many movies; Lisa's guidance counselor doesn't want to get involved, either, so her three friends decide to try to drag Lisa back from the edge of the mental cliff she's heading for. .

Anyway, the conversation had moved into a discussion of parents in general and what the duty of "real" friends is...both topics Sandi had presented to the kids.

By the end of that period, students had shared moments of agony regarding their parents and had gotten into a major discussion about what a "real" friend was.

"But when the bell rang—an' this was seventh period, Tom—they all went 'aww' and no one—not a single one of them got up to leave! Tom, they wanted to stay and keep talkin' to each other. Tom, two of the girls were cryin' and tellin' each other how much they needed them as friends...and...oh God, Tom, what a moment! I had tears runnin' down my cheeks when I told 'em we'd continue the talk the next day. Tom, little Megan Curtin, who hardly ever said a word up till then, came up to me as they were leavin' and hugged me, cryin', and told me that it was the most meaningful class she'd ever been in! Tom, now I know what you meant. God, it was such a *magic moment!*" she gasped as she leaned back against the sofa and wiped her eyes with the back of her hands.

I'd hugged her and held her, as I whispered, "Think you could have that experience selling insurance or bein' an accountant...or even teachin' math? This is why we're doin' it, my goddess, this is why," I whispered as I stroked her lustrous blond hair and kissed the top of her head.

I was destined to have my magic moment a little later in the year...well, much later, actually.

I had *my* magical moment in teaching with a class, that year, my one senior English class. It wasn't small; maybe there were twenty-four kids in it, way too large, but not large enough to break into two. The personalities were all over the place, in every possible type—quiet ones, crazy ones, troubled ones, happy ones, ones who spread happiness, even one or two cynical ones, already like Holden and unwilling to believe any adults were what they claimed to be.

Donny, whom I had dubbed "The Mystery Man" on the first day of class the year before because he'd come in with a friend, Jimmie (yeah, the same Donny and Jimmie from the previous years' creative-writing class), but had just listened to me talk to Jimmie and hadn't said a word, thus the "Mystery Man" part; Donny, whose hair color and appearance changed weekly...and Donny, who'd never acted in a play before and blew us away as Tevya when the kids put on *Fiddler on the Roof* that spring.

Jimmie, a recent transfer the year before from northeastern Virginia, near Washington, still trying to get over culture shock from moving to a county populated more by cattle and trees than people.

Arabella, whose self-esteem had been destroyed the year before in junior English by a teacher who judged his standards by how many kids he could give D's and F's to. I remember meeting Arabella's father at the National Honor Society induction; he sounded like that Southern colonel from a Bugs Bunny cartoon, with his slow, Southern drawl:

"Mr. Finn, Ah'm Lloyd Tippett, and I'd like to thank you, suh, fo' bringin' my little girl back to someone we once knew. Her beliefs in herself were destroyed by her previous English teacher. She now believes in herself again, and we thank you."

I told the father that I understood, because in high school, my best friend's sister had had the same kind of teacher for two years, and since she had refused to brown-nose him, as many other of his personal "A" students had, he'd been responsible for giving her the only B she'd received in four years of high school—for a numerical average of *94.8*! That particular teacher had smugly stated to the sister—and later, to the parents—that "there is no written policy that I have to round your average up to the next number." I went on to tell the father that if that B had kept Maria out of the University of Pennsylvania, Tony and I had planned to take that teacher out to the woods and to beat him to within an inch of his life. Mr. Tippett smiled slowly, and then replied, "Suh, with those kinds of vermin, I would consider that a great waste of yo' energy."

He shook my hand once more, a warm, dry, strong handshake, and then went to enjoy the NHS reception. Arabella, with whom I shared my strawberries; Arabella, who once got the nickname of "Headlights" from Donny and Jimmie when we were reading *Our Town* until she threatened to beat the two of them to a pulp.

Jess, who had rebelled against her domineering parents by purposefully getting pregnant the year before, as a junior, and was now a senior and a mother.

Cassie, who let passion get the better of her and who came to me in her senior year—and her second year with me—curled herself in my lap and cried because she couldn't bear my disappointment when she told me that she, too, was pregnant. They took away her senior-class presidency and her title of Miss Luray when word got out. A wounded bird who still calls me on Father's Day to tell me she loves me more than her divorced dad in Texas. Cassie, still a mother but without a man who deserves her.

…and a lot more….

They came to class….they debated incessantly…I watched the girls in the class become more and more assertive as I pushed them to hold their own against the overly opinionated boys…they joined me and The Lunch Bunch some times to continue the debates that had started in my class…or in government class…

…and on the second-to-last day of my second school year, they had sat in a circle and had talked, openly and honestly, about how they felt about each other, and about what they had experienced in what Paul had called "the most unbelievably different and amazing English class in the history of the world," and yes, about how they felt about me, using up an entire box of tissues.

…and on the last half-day of school, as the final bell rang at eleven that morning, they had all stood on top of their desks to applaud me, as they had seen in Robin Williams' *Dead Poets' Society*.

I will never forget that moment: my door was open, and as students were dashing past outside to leave for the summer, one of them glanced through to see all these seniors standing on desks, clapping their hands. Other kids in the hall stopped to watch, while even more crashed into the rear of the ever-increasing crowd outside, not expecting to find anyone stopping inside school on the last day.

I will never forget little, skinny Addison, her slender legs in baggy shorts, looking down at me and crying…or Clare, smiling insanely…or little Jess, her dark eyes filled with tears…or Donny and Jimmie, who had obviously planned the whole thing, wiping their own tears away…until I had said "All right, enough, enough!" through my own tears and they began to step down onto the floor of room 213.

I can still feel Arabella's arms around my neck as she gave my cheek a kiss and whispered, "Thanks, T., I love you. I wish I was older or you were younger."

After they had all gone, I turned off the lights in my room and cried. I'm not sure why. I think it was for a good reason, but sometimes I think it's because I didn't ever want them to leave, I didn't want to say goodbye to them a few days later at graduation.

On that last day of school, a beautiful June day when every native tulip tree in Page County was amazingly still in bloom, I'd driven us and Baby home when I saw it coming up ahead.

WELCOME TO LURAY, VIRGINIA
Established 1812
Visit or Stay

I pulled the Camaro over onto the shoulder of the highway, shifted into neutral, and put on the brake. She turned and looked at me strangely.

"What?" she asked.

I didn't say anything; I just got out, went around to her side, opened the door, and dragged her out. She laughed a little.

"Tom, what are you doin'?"

I walked us over until we were under the sign.

"See this sign?" I asked.

"Yeah, so what? What, we see it every day," she said, beginning to frown.

I just kissed her; I kissed her hard and long, bending her back a little and holding the back of her head tightly. A couple vehicles went by at the time; a pickup beeped long and hard as well. When I was done, I stood her back up straight.

"Wha...what are you doin'?!" she asked, half flushed and half embarrassed, I think.

"This sign greeted me a year ago. Last Christmas, I decided to ask you to marry me because I had decided to stay. If I'd never come here, I wouldn't have the great kids to teach, I wouldn't have a father who's happier than he's been in two years, I wouldn't have the little sister I always wished I had, and I certainly wouldn't have you. This damn sign is like my Star of Bethlehem—it led me here, to you. I love you. And I love the fact that you're a teacher. And I am *never* going to get tired of loving you...or making love to you. All because of this sign. *That's* what I'm doin'!"

WELCOME TO LURAY, VIRGINIA
Established 1812
Visit or Stay

"Bigots and hypocrites aside, we're gonna stay. God has led me to where I belong, and the person I belong with...and there's a lot more than one. Thank you, Lord. I'll try to do what you led me here to do. I'm young but I'm learning. Thank you for this place, these people, this beautiful goddess next to me. Thanks," I said aloud as more traffic went by. They probably wondered what we were doing there, but I didn't care so I didn't look.

I looked down at her, instead; the blue eyes were wide, the tears on her cheeks were happy tears, I knew...yeah, I was where I was supposed to be.

And yeah, teaching...what a marvelous and emotionally exhausting profession. And we'll keep coming back to do it one more time. And maybe *next* year, I can just teach.